All the Horses of Iceland

ALL THE HORSES OF ICELAND

SARAH TOLMIE

A TOM DOHERTY ASSOCIATES BOOK

NEW YORK

ALL THE HORSES OF ICELAND

Edited by Carl Engle-Laird

Cover art by Erin Vest
Cover design by Christine Foltzer

A Tordotcom Book
Published by Tom Doherty Associates
120 Broadway
New York, NY 10271

www.tor.com

Tor® is a registered trademark of Macmillan Publishing Group, LLC.

ISBN 978-1-250-80794-6 (ebook)
ISBN 978-1-250-80793-9 (trade paperback)

First Edition: 2022

To my mother, Ruth MacKenzie Tolmie

All the Horses of Iceland

EVERYONE KNOWS THE STORY OF THE MARE SKALM.
How she lay down with her pack still on, and Seal Thorir founded his farm in that place. It says so in *Landnámabók*. Skalm was wise. This is the story of another horse, one even more deserving of fame, though she has no name. This mare's story proves that one can be famous without a name, a valuable lesson. She is the most famous of all the horses of Iceland.

She is all the horses of Iceland.

People tell many strange lies about the horses of Iceland. How they are made of fire that has leached into their bones from the fiery earth, or sky that they have sucked into their lungs from the tops of mountains. So there are sorrel horses, and horses with blue eyes. How a great stallion was once caught in a crevasse, caught by his near fore- and hind leg, while his off legs kept running and running, scrabbling on the ice for a foothold until he pulled himself out, sweating and steaming with effort. So ever after he ran using his legs first on the one side, then the other, and the tölt was born.

The truth about them is scarcely less strange. Every horse in Iceland, like every person, has ancestors who sailed here in a ship. What has a horse to do with a ship? In a ship, a horse cannot hold on. A horse cannot row or trim sail or bail out water. A horse has no business on the sea at all. Horses were carried here, cold and sick and protesting, in open boats, frost riming their manes, from Norvegr and the Føroyar, from Irland and Hjaltland and the Suthreyar. Their sturdy kin can be seen in all those places, long-haired in winter, working around farms and fjords. These little horses of the North, strong as oxen, carry tall men in their endeavours of work and pleasure and war, all the way to Garthariki. The mare of whom this saga speaks, she came from a land beyond even these, a great ocean of grass. Her journey here was long and the wealth she brought with her was considerable, but no rune stones speak of them. What are the most important words, after all, that rune stones record?

Names.

When Eyvind of Eyri left the island of Iceland in the prime of his life he was already an old man. He could not have children. It is not that he was impotent, but he could produce no offspring. He was also deaf in one ear. As a child, he had had the throat-swelling fever. It is seen that people who survive this fever often have such defects. But he was young and strong. He went as a crewman on a knarr trading, as he thought, to Grikkland. He hoped to see Miklagarth. But that is not what happened.

There are many tales of wide-travellers. Many are about war. Some are about trade. Many are about war, then trade. Some are about trade, then war. Eyvind's tale is different. He passed through many lands that were at war: lands in which retainers were murdering their lords, lands being overrun by neighbours or by strangers, lands newly taken and rebellious, lands in which not so much as a single grape was left hanging on a vine. He saw villages in cinders. He saw rich towns in which men sat in comfort reading books with golden covers. Eyvind coveted the books, and not only for the gold. He understood that treasures also lay inside the covers, treasures that were hard to put a price on. While Eyvind never became a literate man, he saw as he went on that books contained words that could transform men into priests and kings and healers.

By now you may think that Eyvind's story concerns his conversion, as do so many stories from the pagan time. And while it is true that the lands through which he passed were rife with priests of every kind, and that as he went on he encountered Christians and Sarks and Jews before any of these religions had been heard of in Iceland, nonetheless he did not convert. None of these faiths appealed to him and he died as pagan as he was born. I, Jór, cannot approve of this. Yet the fact remains that in the matter of religion he was no better and no worse than the rest of his countrymen during the period of the settlement. Many books here in the library at Skálaholt attest to this, even those concerning the behaviour of great men at the time of the kristnitaka such as Thorgeir Thorkellsson.

It was the conversion of his captain, the merchant Ingwe Blakkr, that first drove Eyvind from his ship and companions. Ingwe, who was unscrupulous and beginning to be rich, accepted baptism in order to impress the chieftain Oleg, ruler of Helmgard, whose mother Olga was a Christian. Olga was powerful in Oleg's house, and Ingwe assumed that her influence would prevail. In this he proved correct. Oleg converted and accepted baptism from a Greek bishop. Thereafter he declared he would trade only with Christians, putting Ingwe and his men in a favourable position. The majority of the men on the knarr agreed with Ingwe and declared themselves Christians, though only a few of them underwent the ritual. Eyvind would not do so.

"If your captain becomes a Christian, you become a Christian also," said Ingwe.

"No," said Eyvind. In this he was quite right. Any man of God will tell you that this is not how one becomes a Christian. God is greater than kings or captains. Nor should we seek to buy our way into his mercy. In Iceland, when the conversion came, it came to everyone at once as a matter of agreement and so that all Icelanders should remain under one law. Thorgeir the gothi lay flat upon the ground all the night through, meditating, and when he cast off his fur cape in the morning he declared in favour of the God of the Gospels. As he had been duly appointed lawspeaker, it was a binding agreement. God is not divorced from reason. What temptations Thorgeir might have endured, and what the divine voice might have said to him in the darkness of that night, he never said, though many priests since have attributed to him a mighty visitation, an epiphany such as was experienced by the first disciples. None have said that Ingwe experienced any such visitation.

"Then leave," said Ingwe to Eyvind.

"I will," said Eyvind. Ingwe paid him what he was owed. He had been a fellow in the journey, laying his money down with the rest. Three other men with whom Eyvind was friendly, none of whom had been baptized, stood with him as he received his payment. Eyvind thanked them and left the crew. He had no dealings with Icelanders after that for four years.

Eyvind went out alone into the city of Helmgard. It was high summer. He considered what he would do. He had money. He could buy in to another trading vessel. He went to the market square, where it was too hot and the meat was stinking. With a practiced eye he quickly found the stall of the most substantial merchant there, one who was selling leather and cloth, cord and ribbon, and many stoppered vessels of clay that he assumed must be filled with something or other that was precious. He spoke to this man, who was shorter than he and had black hair and black eyes. He was in his middle years, as his hair was greying. Young men rarely commanded so much wealth. The man wore a long dark robe with red stitching at the sleeves and a small fur hat. His hair was cut to his shoulders and fell straight, without a wave, and he had no beard. Nonetheless, he appeared authoritative. Eyvind asked him whither he was bound after this market. Did he trade on the river or elsewhere? How large was his operation? Had he any need of a man who could invest a small sum?

The merchant did not reply at once. He looked as if he were mulling things over. Eyvind wondered if he had spoken in the right language. There were many languages in the city, and Eyvind did not speak any of them exactly. He addressed the man using the river-language of the region, in words that were not precisely those of Iceland, nor of Norvegr, but that resembled that tongue except in having many foreign words thrown in. The words that Eyvind did not know natively he assumed came from the language of the other men of Helmgard, of whom there were many—indeed, the majority. These were large men with fair skin and pointed noses, with hair of various colours, who wore heavy furs. Some had blue eyes, some brown. They owned houses and docks and taverns and were part of the chieftain's council. They were brotherly and went about together, speaking among themselves this language that Eyvind did not know, though they all spoke the river-language, too. They spoke it in Oleg's house, for instance. The man to whom Eyvind was speaking did not look like these men at all. His skin was darker and his nose less prominent, its bridge not extending far beyond his cheekbones. Eyvind wondered if he had made a mistake. But he did not know any other languages and the man was here to trade. Traders have to talk. So Eyvind waited.

Finally the merchant said, "I am not a river-trader. Not primarily. Most of my destinations are far inland. We travel not by ship but by *ät* or *tebe*."

Eyvind did not know either of the words the man used to express how he travelled. *Ship* he could understand. "*Ät?*" he said. "*Tebe?*"

"*Ät*," replied the man, and he neighed most accurately.

"Horse," said Eyvind, nodding. "*Tebe*?"

The man opened his mouth and made a groaning roar that conveyed nothing to Eyvind at all. It might have been a cow or a woman in labour. An ox, perhaps? He shrugged his incomprehension. The man made a slight, dismissive gesture, flicking his hand as if to ward off flies.

"Where do you go by horse? Inland? How far? Which way?" asked Eyvind.

"South," replied the man, "and east."

"To Sarkland?"

"Beyond Sarkland. To the steppes. Men there are not Arabs, or Persians, or Khitans, or Khazars. They speak a language unlike others."

"I do not know all those peoples," admitted Eyvind. "For what items do you trade in this place?"

"Horses. Hides. Herbs. Butter of mare's milk."

"How long is the journey?"

"Between one hundred days and a year. It depends."

"On what does it depend? Weather?"

"War. Our caravans must pass through Khazaria, a great land, an empire with many clients, many peoples. We—Khazars—control many of the trade routes in this region and exact tolls. We have been warring with the Rus now for many years. We began to lose ground in the time of my father. The father of Oleg, Vladimir, he crushed two of our cities in the year of the rabbit—Samandar and

Balangar. No matter. We are building a great fortress at Sarkel. The Khazars are far from subdued. Much of their land is laid waste but much is still fertile. There is a saying among Khazars: 'a man with three horses is an army.'"

"We would say much the same in Iceland," observed Eyvind.

"There is a land of ice?"

"Yes," said Eyvind, "an island beyond Hålogaland but not so far as Groenland. There are farms round the edges, ice on the heights, and a fiery plain in the middle. An island of black rock and independent people."

"In the north of the steppes where the tribes of Tungusk live—they breed good horses—it is cold enough to freeze a man's eyes. Your breath falls solid ice from your mouth. Is it as cold as that?"

"Yes," said Eyvind, proudly.

"What is your name?" asked the black-eyed man. It was appropriate for him to ask this, as Eyvind had asked him for work.

"Eyvind."

"What does it mean?"

"Island-wind."

The merchant looked at him with growing interest. "I am David," he said.

Eyvind looked back at him. "Christians have that name," he said.

"Christians have that name because Jews had it before them," replied the man, David. "Christians steal everything."

"To whom do you sell your horses?" asked Eyvind.

"Khazars," said David.

"And here you sell hides and cord?"

"And mare's butter," replied David.

"When do you depart?" asked Eyvind.

"This market lasts five more days," the man replied. "I never stay in Helmgard longer than necessary."

"I will go with you if you need a man who pays his way and expects return. I can ride a horse—*ät*," said Eyvind.

"Can you ride a *tebe*?" asked David.

"We will have to see," said Eyvind.

David had said that he was not a river-trader, but still he and his party journeyed for many weeks along the great river that he called the Itil. They carried with them a cargo of iron bits and bridle fittings, arrowheads, wheat flour, and strong brandy. Eyvind saw that he was angry at having to pay tithes to Rus lords along the way, but still he did so. He said to Eyvind, "Soon enough it will be Khazars we pay, the closer we come to Itil, the great port that controls entry to the Khazar Sea. These flyspeck towns, Aldeigjuborg, Helmgard and the like, they do not deserve the name of city. In Itil, you will see a true city. Indeed, it is three cities, stretching right across the river at its widest point: one for the merchants, one for the nobility, and the sacred city of the king."

"The king has his own city?" said Eyvind.

"Yes," said David. "No-one ever sees it, or him. He is holy."

"How then does he rule, if the people never see him?"

"He is holy," repeated David. "It is best that holy things not be seen."

"Has he his family with him, then? His women? Servants?"

"Oh yes, there is a great household. His kin and wives and servants, and many of his guards from Khwarazem. They live in a palace on an island in the centre of the river. A most holy place. Only nobles ever set foot there, at certain prescribed times, to check on him."

"Where is Khwarazem? He is protected by foreign guards?" To Eyvind this seemed unwise.

"A Persian land near the Sea of Islands. They are great horsemen, newly converted to Islam. The *bäk* draws his elite guard from there. He pays them in silver. It is safer than relying on the nobility."

"It is?"

"His nobles will be the ones to kill him. Eventually,

at the prescribed time. But perhaps some of them might want to get it done early, and choose another king."

Eyvind found this baffling. "You mean to say, there is a scheduled uprising? And high-born men kill their own chieftain?"

"Not an uprising. A sacrifice. The *bäk* serves the people for a prescribed time. Then he is killed and replaced by another. His body is buried with great ceremony under running water. It is then, to speak truly, that he is at his most powerful. Every *bäk* so buried is a bulwark to his people, an ancestor to call on and a protector of the homeland."

"This is remarkable," said Eyvind. "And the *bäk* agrees to do this?"

"Indeed, he chooses the number of years for which he will rule. Or so it is said. I would not know. These secrets are known only to the noble rank, the king-tribes. Those who can approach the island."

"Who runs the army of the Khazars, then? This strong army of which you speak, that fights the Rus?"

"The *qagan-bäk*, the lieutenant king. Today this man is Alp Tarkhan. The *bäk* is Nisi Ben Manasseh. That is a Hebrew name."

"Things are marvellous in Khazaria," said Eyvind. "You told me that this is the language of Jews? I thought they lived far from here, in southern lands? In Sarkland, as a subject people? Are there not Jews in the Christians' book?"

"There are Jews in the Jews' book," said David, shortly.

"Your *bäk* is Jewish, then?"

"He is," replied David, "and so is his court. Many nobles. Some merchants. Myself, for instance. But not everyone in the empire, by any means. Not even Alp Tarkhan. There are many religions here. We in Khazaria are caught in a trap of God: Christians to the north and west of us and Sarks to the south. Those of us who prefer one God have chosen the God of the Hebrews. He is very old and we prefer old things. I have heard old men say that the God of the Israelites, whose name is not to be uttered aloud, is like the ancient Kōk Tengri, the god of the blue sky. He is widely worshipped here and right across the steppes, as far north as Bjarmland."

"I despise gods," said Eyvind. "I see no need for them. Men, animals, ghosts, and luck. That is what the world is composed of."

"But who makes the luck?" asked David.

"The interactions of men, ghosts, and animals."

"Then why are there priests of one kind or another wherever you go?" asked David.

"I have often wondered that. Some men are good talkers. Some men are good at solemnity. People need this as much as food. They admire such men as much as they admire warriors. It is odd."

"In many lands hereabouts the priests are women," said David. "Or so you might call them. Magicians. Among the Bulghurs and the people of Tungusk and many other tribes, women are healers and travellers to the spirit world, along with the men. In the far land towards which we are going they are known as *udugan*."

"It is even more ridiculous when the priests are women," replied Eyvind. "It is so in many places in Iceland and Svealand and especially in Gotaland. Women who carry distaffs—all women carry them, so what?—and perform *seithr*. It is unmanly nonsense."

"There are no women priests in Judaism," said David.

"That makes sense, at least," said Eyvind.

Eyvind looked forward to seeing the wonderful city of the Khazars. But when they were five days' journey from Itil, they were stopped by war. Boats flying back upriver carried men who shouted in many languages that a huge army had marched out from Sarkel and engaged a combined force of Greeks and Rus (as both were now Christian) that had been heading for Itil. All the plains between were fields of slaughter. Armies had burned crops and towns and taken many slaves. The final result was not yet known. David prudently unloaded his cargo at the first settlement he came to and bought a train of packhorses. He sold his boat casually, without ceremony. Eyvind was shocked. He got on the gelding that David gave him—a roan with a drooping ear and a smooth gait—and he and David's party, twenty-six men in all, rode east, away from the river and the battle.

———————

It is difficult to take the magic of foreign lands seriously. Christian authorities are severe upon scribes that we should not waste time and vellum recording pagan activities. They are not wrong. Nevertheless I intend to continue to speak of Eyvind and The Mare With No Name, as they are part of the history of Iceland and of the important region of Eyri. Eyvind brought back with him, along with the mare, a certain document. I, Jór, have seen it here in the library at Skálaholt. It is written in some kind of handsome rune with which I am not familiar, ordered in vertical columns. The strokes of these runes intersect with great complexity, and they include curved lines not suitable for carving, and not easily made with a quill. These runes have been glossed by some hand in Greek, in clumps of hurried characters. These also I cannot read. Fortunately, another, finer hand has glossed this Greek—so I assume—in fine Latin uncials. I would like to congratulate that man, as his script is beautiful. So the text runs:

In the year of the rabbit, the people of Sorqan Šira, he having been raised as qan, were camped on the banks of the Onan. There they were plagued by a ghost. The qan had taken into the company of his principal wives Bortë, daughter of Tarqutai Kiriltuq. Her mother was Hoë'lün of the Ol'qunu'ut and she came of a long line of white magicians of high rank. Bortë of the beautiful cheeks was seated one evening at the rear of the tent facing the door—she was known to have kindled her first child—when she suddenly pitched over on her face, dead. Women screamed. They feared she had been poisoned. Her body was removed from the tent as soon as possible. It was buried in the ground and the qan's most powerful magician poured a libation. He remained there all night with his horse skin drum. The people performed appropriate sacrifices for the dead. Nonetheless it soon became clear that Bortë was not resting peacefully. Night after night she appeared in the tent, sitting among the women in her accustomed place. The fire gave less warmth when she was there. Two of the qan's women miscarried, perhaps from fear, perhaps from magic. None of the qan's principal magicians could get her to go. Finally they appealed to Bortë's mother and sent a cart a long way to fetch her. She arrived with her drum and her ceremonial robe and a leather bag of fresh curds for an offering. She begged permission from the qan to sit in his place in the tent. "I will try to trick her that way," she said. He agreed reluctantly. So the mother, Hoë'lün, sat in the place of the qan as women, slaves, and retainers filed in and sat down. The qan stood by the door, facing inward. In such a shameful position, Hoë'lün said, the ghost would not even see him. At this he was hardly pleased. They waited for Bortë to appear. Soon enough she did, flowing in through the tent hole. She lowered herself in, climbing hand and foot down the column of blue smoke until she stood on the floor. "Hello, Mother," she said, and stepped on to the qan's white rug. She looked towards the door. "Hello, my husband," she said. "This is a strong ghost," said Hoë'lün, "without respect for rules." She stood up and went to sit among the principal wives and invited Bortë to join her. The qan returned to his own place in anger. Hoë'lün threw so many magic herbs in the fire that the tent became filled with yellow smoke and many people ran out coughing and retching. Those who remained could hardly see. Nor could they hear anything, but the women sitting nearest to Bortë and her mother reported that their lips moved soundlessly for a long time, when they could see them through the smoke. Eventually the smoke cleared. Bortë was gone and the bag of curds with her. Her mother sat there alone with red-rimmed eyes. She said to the qan, "This is how the situation stands. My daughter is stuck between worlds. She was carrying a magic child, a strong one, full of life, when she died. The child's soul has pulled her wind horse, the soul of her flesh, too firmly into this world for it to let go. Her free soul, as you have seen, is able to move about. It would prefer to depart. Not even Bortë is happy with this." "What can we do?" asked the qan. "You might summon a great magician, one of an ancient line, and see if he can do anything," said the mother. "But Bortë seems to think it will not avail. She has an intuition that only foreign magic will suffice, and that soon enough a stranger will come who has some. Meanwhile, if you provide her with a regular supply of curds and allow her near the fire every ninth night she will trouble you but little." The qan instructed his women to do this. He rewarded the magician Hoë'lün with a fine dun gelding with a dorsal stripe and she departed. All went as well as it might until a rebellious and hungry concubine began stealing Bortë's curds. When this was discovered the qan executed her but the damage was done. From that time onward Bortë was seen less often in her own person, but animal after animal in the qan's herds—sometimes horses, sometimes cattle—went crazy. They ran themselves to death. Cattle gored people. Horses fought with dogs. Their eyes rolled and they drooled unnaturally. The horses' tails emitted a green glow. The qan moved his camp three times. Every time the ghost found them.

Eyvind learned to ride a *tebe,* a smelly and fierce animal with splayed feet and a great mound of flesh in the middle of the back, inconveniently placed. He did not love them. He preferred horses. After a long matter of months and trading in many towns, he and David's party came to a great ocean of tough grass. It went on and on to the horizon, waving like the sea. Had Eyvind not been a sailor already it would have made him sea-sick. He spent many hours staring down at the neck of his smooth-gaited roan—he had determinedly hung on to this horse despite many trading opportunities—so as to keep his head from spinning when he looked at the great distances. Sailors likewise spend much time doing close tasks for this reason.

"We have come to the country of the *udugan,*" said David. "There are many kings here, greater and lesser, who govern tribes of their own people and enslave others so that they have plenty of people to work. Nonetheless they are great traders. Do not offend anybody who calls himself qan and you can make plenty of money here."

"But there is nothing here except grass," replied Eyvind. "Mind you, we could use some of this grass in

Iceland. It is an improvement on bare rock. Men could farm here."

"Yet men do not farm here. The grass has tough roots and the weather is dreadful. There is not enough water to maintain crops."

"Surely there are lakes?"

"There are lakes. Great ones, like Lake Tengiz, and small ones. Some are brackish. Some are freezing cold. Some, they say, are haunted. Any tribe near a lake will keep it from all others."

"So then there is water to farm," said Eyvind, "if people would just work hard enough. Or co-operate, or make better laws."

"Do not say so to a *qan*," replied David. "Besides, you will find they have plenty of laws."

"That is some comfort," said Eyvind. "Still, a land without farmers is a poor land. Farming is the most important profession of all."

"Why aren't you a farmer, then?" asked David.

"Did I say I was a great man?" said Eyvind. "Besides, I can't afford it."

"After this you may be able to," said David, "provided that you remember that here herdsmen and shepherds are chieftains."

"At home, herdsmen and shepherds are scum. Idiots and hired help. As bad as reindeer-herders," replied

Eyvind. "Fortunately, there are no reindeer in Iceland. Foolish, wasteful animals, worse than *tebe*."

"Keep your mouth shut about it," advised David.

Not long after this they rode into a village of tents. Some of the tents were very big and impressed Eyvind considerably. Some had streamers of red and blue flying on poles beside them. The largest had discs of shiny metal or glass sparkling upon it, dizzying in the sun. Eyvind and the other men dismounted, and faces appeared quickly as flaps opened in the tents. The faces appeared to Eyvind to resemble David's: small-featured, broad-cheeked, though few of them wore head coverings, as David always did. David ignored the appearing faces and inclined his body in a silent bow towards the largest of the tents, the one with the shiny discs.

Eyvind took several steps towards the large tent.

"Stop," said David.

Before Eyvind could respond in any way, ten men who had not been there before appeared out of the grass where they had been lying, encircling the large tent. It was as if they grew out of the ground. They made no sound whatsoever. All were armed with bows; five drew, five waited. Eyvind stepped back slowly, watching them.

"If you walk between the tent guards, or even come

abreast of them, they will kill you," said David. "That is one of their laws."

"I see," said Eyvind.

At that moment the tent flap opened, and was held open, by an elderly man. The man looked at David, and David bowed to him. The man inclined his head briefly and gestured through the flap. David immediately handed off his horse to another man. Saying to Eyvind, "Come!" he walked fearlessly through the door. Eyvind followed. He noticed as he went close by the flap that it was made, not of hide as he had assumed, but of cloth. Elements of the tent were made of hides, he saw, but most of it was made of this same thick, matte, uniform cloth, enormous swathes of it. There was little visible stitching and no warp or weft. It was a complete mystery. How it had been made he could not tell. It appeared magical.

Once inside the tent Eyvind was uncomfortable for a number of reasons. It was dark compared to the bright light outside. The air smelled of smoke from a smoored fire at the centre, from which small tendrils curled towards an opening at the top of the tent. A surprising number of people, men and women, were ranged around it, seated on the floor on many rich rugs. His eye instantly understood that there was a nuanced order among them, but he did not know what it was. There were two wooden benches, one on each side of the door. David motioned him to sit on one of them. He did so. In a chieftain's house, as a rule, a bench or any place of elevation is a place of honour. Eyvind sensed that the same was not so here. Nor did he like to sit with his back to the door. Perched on his bench, far above the company, he felt like an offering on a pole. It was a most unpropitious location. Worst of all, he was now in a position that no person likes to be in: the only man in a room who does not understand the language being spoken. Opportunities for shame are rife in such a situation. One can become the butt of any man's joke. Eyvind felt many eyes on him and strove to remain impassive despite looks of suspicion, and, it seemed to him, revulsion. He was a man neither good-looking nor vain, but he was not accustomed to being looked at in such a way.

David discoursed for some time in a language that sounded quite different from the one Eyvind had heard him speak in Khazaria. He was impressed by the merchant's facility. A smallish man of middle years who wore the richest clothing, sat nearest the fire, and to whom all deferred, replied ceremoniously. This was the *qan*, Eyvind decided. After some time David glanced over to him and said, "Some of the women think you are an albino. A freak of nature."

Eyvind decided it was best to say nothing.

"The *qan*, however, has seen light-skinned men before,

Rus and others. He is used to them. He will command his folk to tolerate you. Albinos, you should know, are usually killed. They are unlucky. Still, you may find that some people will assume you are blind because of your blue eyes."

"I appreciate your telling me," said Eyvind. He was put out. It was all very well to expose children who were deformed, he thought, but how are blue eyes or pale skin deformities? It was unpleasant to be classed with weaklings.

David's oratory continued for a long time. At a certain point the *qan* sent out a boy, who returned with samples of various wares. Discussion ensued among various parties. Eyvind was formally introduced to the *qan* and bowed to him. The man, Sorqan Šira, looked amused. The two traders were offered food, which consisted mostly of meat, both lamb and horse, and either fresh or fermented cheese that was mixed with water and drunk. These were sour but palatable. David refused the drinks, which Eyvind considered risky, even in a man already known to the *qan*. David claimed that men of his religion preferred to drink water in these circumstances. However, he had another boy sent out to the caravan to fetch some precious brandy, which he offered to the *qan* as a gift. The *qan* accepted eagerly. David kept aside one small vessel of spirits and this he mixed with his water. So all were satisfied. Eyvind relaxed somewhat after he had consumed the food. Rarely will a man kill you directly after he has fed you. It is not polite. The *qan* was pleased to receive an additional gift of wheat flour, with which commodity he also seemed familiar. He elaborately praised the gifts he had been given to his wives and entrusted them to their care. Eyvind understood that they had received permission to trade.

———————

The *qan* assigned a boy of about nine winters and an old woman to Eyvind, in order to help him learn the language. They became his personal property. Though the *qan* had many bondspeople and this was no hardship for him, Eyvind appreciated the gesture all the same. After a length of time Eyvind understood the wisdom of this choice, as there is nothing that a child of nine and an old woman, between them, cannot teach you about village life. Matters of trade, such as men discuss, he learned about from David. Soon enough Eyvind was on the lookout for horses.

He noticed that in a land of such superb horse handlers and riders—he saw feats of riding and shooting such as he would never have imagined and was glad that these terrible men lived so far from Iceland—the *qan*'s herds were curiously unruly. Now and again he would see a single animal foaming and rearing and going berserk. Sometimes it would attack people or trample tents. Often this animal was simply shot in the spine and killed, without anyone even trying to tame it. This profligacy was shocking to Eyvind. The mad beasts were often young, healthy animals otherwise. And when they were dead they were not eaten, or even skinned. He assumed it was some sort of sacrifice.

Finally he asked the old woman about it. "Those horses," he said to her, "the ones who go crazy from time to time. I have never seen animals behave that way. Is it some disease?"

"No," said the old woman.

"Where I come from," went on Eyvind, "we would say they were entrolled."

"What is that?" asked the old woman.

"Under the influence of a bad magic," replied Eyvind, feeling foolish. He did not usually discuss trolls. It is best not to. Still, he did not want to purchase troll-ridden horses.

"Where you come from," said the old woman cautiously, "are there magicians who can stop this from happening?"

"I have no idea," replied Eyvind. "I am no magician. David has told me that you have powerful magicians here. Has the *qan* not appealed to them?"

"He has," said the old woman, and she would say no more. The boy followed their conversation with interest.

"It is Bortë, old mother, you know that," he said. "Why do you not say so?"

"Bortë?" repeated Eyvind.

"Wife of the *qan*. Her ghost will not settle. She has been dead two years," said the boy.

Many things then became clear to Eyvind. For a man so wealthy and revered, the *qan* looked tired and dismal. Misfortune hung around his camp. In the time they had been there, few other traders had come. David had re-marked that goods were fewer and men angrier than they had been when he had traded here before. Nobody prospers with a ghost around. It came into Eyvind's mind that he should tell David and his fellows of this. Jews, like everyone else, must surely be troubled by ghosts. Then they could all move on to another settlement.

Before he could speak to David, however, the ghost came to speak to him in his tent. This did not go well. Eyvind barely spoke the language. Her voice was faint and windy and most of the time her lips moved soundlessly. This annoyed him. He kept trying to get close to her so that he could see her face clearly. He could not reach her, though it was a very small tent. It struck him that she was evasive for a ghost. In Iceland, ghosts are robust. Mostly they just clobber you. He had always been terrified by any mention of ghosts when he was a boy—at the people they beat black and blue and the goods they stole and the fertile valleys they sequestered for their own use. What use did they have for such property, anyway? That was the thing about ghosts. They were utterly senseless. So he raged inwardly as he chased the ghost of the *qan*'s wife round and round his small fire. Finally he gave up and sat down. Eventually Bortë came and sat opposite him. He saw her face, pale and sad, across the flames and his heart was filled with desolation. She was not an angry ghost as he had expected. She talked on and on, looking at him with dark eyes. He heard once the word for *male child*, once, he thought, the word *cut*, and many times, *horse*. Horse. Brown horse. Horse. Her hands described an arc in the air, flowing outward, upward, away from her breastbone, then sliced off abruptly. Cut. Horse. Cut. Eyvind watched her with an increasing compassion but remained unsure what to do. To deal with ghosts you must be a magician or a lawyer and he was neither. At dawn, she left, climbing up the column of smoke from his fire as if climbing a ladder. Eyvind thought this was clever but was relieved to see her disappear out the smoke hole. Ghosts, he found, are tiring. He slept thereafter for an entire day and a night and had vivid dreams of wind and fire.

When he awoke he sought out David, told him of these strange events, and requested that the merchant accompany him to see the *qan*. David advised him fervently against this course. He wanted nothing to do with an *udugan*, or, worse, the ghost of an *udugan*. He recommended that Eyvind not get mixed up in magical business. "Do not presume to advise the *qan* on matters of his own religion. He has priests for that and you know nothing about it," he told him.

"What does a ghost have to do with religion?" asked Eyvind. "Death is the other half of life. It happens to everyone. It makes no matter what gods they believe in."

"It matters what gods they obey, and what priests can invoke them. In death or life. Don't be a fool, Eyvind," replied David. He refused to go and talk to the *qan* about anything pertaining to Bortë.

Nonetheless, Eyvind went to talk to the *qan* about her. He took the boy with him, as he was perfectly willing. He was a speedier translator than the old woman, anyway. She would not come. The idea evidently terrified her.

As soon as he was in the great tent with the *qan*, Eyvind began to doubt himself. He looked briefly to his companion but there was not much help to be had from a boy of nine. To him the prospect of a ghost was merely exciting. Eyvind, looking at the boy and remembering his own fear and joy and shame at the magical stories of ghosts and trolls that he knew from his childhood, suddenly decided on the course he would take.

"I have come"—he indicated to the boy that he should translate, and then thought no more about it—"to speak about the ghost of your wife, Bortë. She has just appeared to me, and I understand that she has been possessing animals."

The *qan* made no move but looked exceedingly dangerous.

"Among my people, meddling with magic is considered effeminate. Nonetheless, in order to secure my trading relationships, I am prepared to offer advice. I will only do so, of course, if you, the *qan*, are prepared to accept it. As this is, in the end, a professional matter, I understand that the *qan* might first wish to consult his own magicians," said Eyvind.

The *qan* did not speak for some time. Then he offered a few clipped words to the boy. The child stepped forward importantly and said, "The *qan* will send for you tomorrow." Eyvind withdrew.

He had some idea of the feverish negotiations that must have preceded the meeting that he was called upon to attend in the *qan*'s tent the following day. He knew that he, Eyvind, had no magical power. Yet he still felt compelled—by a mixture of greed for his own advancement and compassion for the ghost—to act. For the first time, he felt that magicians might occupy an awkward and thankless place in the order of things.

Present were the *qan*, his senior tribal magician, and a deputy *udugan* who was acting in the place of Hoë'lün, the mother of Bortë and the highest-ranking magician available, until she arrived. Fast messengers had been sent to fetch her. Everyone was aware that between-world matters could be time-sensitive. Conditions are prone to decay.

Eyvind began by posing a question, the one that had seemed to him most germane. "What did you do with the body of Bortë?" This appeared to him the most obvious inquiry, one that might reveal simple slip-ups in ritual.

From the tribal magician, and the deputy *udugan*, acting upon professional information, he learned:

—that the body of Bortë, daughter of Tarqutai Kiriltuq and wife of Sorqan Šira, had been inhumed, as befits the flesh of the nobility, which ought not to be cast abroad
—that milk had been placed in her mouth, on the undisturbed earth of the grave site, and upon the finished cairn after burial
—that her face had been covered with white *isgeir* (this was the name of the marvellous warpless and

weftless cloth that had so impressed Eyvind previously)

—that an exorcism had been duly performed and her body sprinkled with juniper needles

—that her body had been touched only by her husband on her death day, given that she had no close kin in the village, and that all others with a role in the burial had worn their clothes reversed while performing their duties

—that her grave had been amply supplied with loose grain

—that funeral-goers had processed three times sunwise around the grave

—that no-one had looked back at the grave site and all had gone home a different way than they had come

Many other details were adduced. The fact that Eyvind wished to ascertain was that all parties felt that protocol had been correctly observed. In the end, after some debate, all witnesses and participants agreed that it had been, to the best of their knowledge. Eyvind saw the wisdom of the steps they had taken. It is clear that the dead must be provided with sustenance and valuables, such that their rank is recognized; at the same time, all possible means must be exercised to obfuscate the pathways between the living and the dead.

Eyvind then inquired if, in their view, it was acceptable to meddle with a corpse after burial.

The *qan* conferred with his magicians and said yes. After all, the bodies of commoners and criminals were simply thrown away onto the steppe, and sometimes cut up beforehand. There was no shame in dismemberment.

Was Bortë's grave site clearly known and marked?

Yes. A number of rites had been enacted there.

Eyvind then said, "When the ghost spoke to me in my tent she kept saying *cut, cut.* This made me think of a ritual that I have heard of, one that may be efficacious against stubborn ghosts. It may be performed by anybody, but is particularly effective if performed by a kinsman of the deceased. It is very simple. Dig the body up, cut off the head, and place it by the buttocks. This creates confusion in the ghost. Then the body may be reinterred. I offer this only as a recommendation."

The *qan* agreed that this remedy should be tried. As Hoë'lün was already on her way, it would be best to wait for her to perform the ritual, as she was both Bortë's kin and a powerful magician in her own right. So they agreed to do this.

The next day Hoë'lün arrived. She was curiously unsurprised to see the foreigner. She displayed no revulsion at his white skin or blue eyes. Indeed, she was both respectful and welcoming. Eyvind wondered why this was so. He could not imagine himself feeling especially hospitable to a stranger who advised him to disturb the bones of one of his kindred. Then Hoë'lün said to him, "Bortë told me that you would come. A stranger with strange magic. She is of the opinion that foreign magic is required to free her from her predicament."

"And you, yourself, take no insult over this?" inquired Eyvind. Few possibilities seemed to him more appalling than a feud with a magician. "I must make it absolutely plain that I myself have not a shred of magical power."

"You may have more power than you know," replied Hoë'lün. "Have you ever had a serious illness?"

"I nearly died of throat-swelling fever as a child," Eyvind admitted.

"Did it leave you with bodily affliction? Scars?" the magician asked.

"I am deaf in one ear."

"That is excellent," she replied. Eyvind failed to see that this was the case. "Such an ear may be able to hear into the spirit world." She looked him over. "What is your age?"

"Five and twenty winters, or thereabouts," said Eyvind.

"You have no child?"

"None that I know of," replied Eyvind. This line of questioning was offensive to him.

"And what is your name?" she asked, finally. "And its meaning?"

"Eyvind. It means wind of the island."

"What island?"

"Iceland, my home."

"And that is far from here, across water?"

"Yes."

Hoë'lün looked very satisfied with these replies. Eyvind was suspicious of her motives. "Shall we go, then, to the grave site to enact the ritual?" he asked. "I will come as a witness."

"Yes," she said, and they set off in a cart. They drove a long way, passing through the *qan*'s herds. He had many fine horses, and today all were calm. Most were brown, but a few were dun or black. His own roan gelding roamed among them. He saw one lone white horse, some distance away. "The *qan* prefers brown horses?" he inquired of Hoë'lün.

"The colour of a horse is immaterial," said Hoë'lün.

"True," said Eyvind. He noticed that the white horse was keeping pace with them, moving steadily through the herd, still at a distance. Such purposeful action in a single animal was unusual.

"That is not the herd stallion, is it, the white horse?" asked Eyvind. "It is coming this way." He pointed.

"No," said Hoë'lün, refusing to look towards it. She

drove on. They left the herd behind. Still the white horse kept pace with them. Eyvind watched its solitary course, but soon it became invisible behind a low ridge. They drove on yet further.

When they came to the grave, a cairn of fist-sized stones bedecked with red and blue streamers, alone on the wide steppe, the white horse was waiting. Eyvind considered this uncanny. He was not pleased. "Do you think Bortë has entrolled this horse—ridden it here?" he said to Hoë'lün.

"What horse?" replied Hoë'lün. "I see only white sky." She never looked in the horse's direction.

Eyvind did not argue. He concluded it was magical business. They got down from the cart, unloaded their tools, and began to exhume the body. Hoë'lün was tireless and strong. Eyvind was soon out of breath, but was ashamed to be outdone by an old woman. He moved rocks and dug into the earth until his palms bled. Gradually the body of Bortë emerged. It was barely decayed. She was recognizable as a well-dressed young woman wearing a white mask.

"Take off the mask," Hoë'lün said, harshly, looking down at her daughter. "I cannot do it."

Eyvind did not want to touch the body, but did as she asked. He saw the face of the woman who had spoken to him in his tent. Her eyes were sunken and her cheeks desiccated, but it was she.

"You must do the beheading," said Eyvind. "It is better performed by family." He handed her the sharp tool he had been using.

Bortë's mother moved forward swiftly, as if fearing to lose her nerve, and chopped several times at the neck, which parted easily. The head broke off. Hoë'lün seized it.

"Place it adjacent to the buttocks," instructed Eyvind. This was easier said than done, as the headless body lay on its back. They were obliged to rotate the whole body. Then Hoë'lün was able to wedge the skull directly behind the buttocks, facing upward.

"Don't you think it should face inward?" said Eyvind.

"She must continue to look up at father sky," said Hoë'lün. "Replace the *isgeir.*"

Eyvind laid the mask of white *isgeir* back over the face. It looked eerie in such a position. As he touched the cloth to Bortë's skin, the white horse gave a terrible scream. Eyvind jumped and fell backward out of the grave. Hoë'lün looked perfectly unconcerned. She glanced at him as he lay on the grass.

"Didn't you hear that?" said Eyvind, shaken. He looked towards the white horse, which had been standing not far off the entire time, gleaming faintly as dusk came on. It was gone.

"What?" asked Hoë'lün.

"The scream of the horse," said Eyvind, fed up with her obtuseness.

"With which ear did you hear this scream?" inquired the magician.

Eyvind could not bear to think of the implications that any answer of his might contain, so he said nothing.

"Night is falling," said Hoë'lün, "so let us hurry and cover her again." They did so. Hoë'lün poured new milk on the grave. Then she and Eyvind returned to the camp.

The *qan*'s tents and herds were quiet for ten days thereafter. When Eyvind returned from the ritual David had said to him, holding up a hand: "Tell me nothing about it. I want nothing to do with this matter." Eyvind, therefore, did not discuss it with him. He waited to see what would transpire. Hoë'lün, he noted, had not yet departed the camp. She, too, was waiting. He did not find this encouraging. The *qan*, however, seemed relieved. He approached Eyvind several days after their return, out in the open where he could not be overheard, and told him that after forty-nine days had elapsed from the reburial—which was, in effect, a second death—they could be certain that the ghost would not reappear. If the tents and herds remained untroubled on the fiftieth day, Eyvind would have earned a huge reward. In the meantime, he gave him a concubine, which was a diversion.

Eyvind continued to learn the language from his nine- and his ninety-year-old tutors. He continued to examine, count, and catalogue potential trade goods. He spent time with his fellow trading companions, who were Khazars like David, though only one other of the twenty-five men professed the Jewish faith. That man, Benjamin, likewise kept his head covered and showed the same aversion to *kumiss* at meals. But most of the time Eyvind spent among the horses. In principle he was evaluating them, seeing which ones he wanted to buy, speculating about which ones he might be given in gift if all turned out well, and so on. But such practical matters were often far from his mind. Eyvind loved horses. He always had. His father's horse Geirr had been his family's prized possession in Eyvind's younger years. He had taken every opportunity to see horses at races and fights, and once had gone with his uncle, who had then been in the market for a foal, to the spring roundup to see the herds come charging down from the mountains like a gale. It was the most remarkable sight he had ever seen. He had dreamed of it for years afterwards.

The *qan* owned more horses than Eyvind had ever seen in one place. In the herd kept close to the camp alone there were over eight hundreds, and he had been told that there were two subsidiary herds kept on higher, remoter ground to toughen them up. Thus the horses were never all in one place if raiders struck. Raids were a regular occurrence among the competing clans. Eyvind spent hours and days wandering, sometimes mounted, sometimes on foot, among the grazing herds. From what he could understand from David, and from herders he met here and there, there were more horses belonging to the clan of the *qan* and to his nearest neighbour, also a powerful chieftain, than there were in all of Iceland. It might be that the *qan* owned more personally. Reckoning them up by talking to herders was difficult. They all counted rapidly in units of ten, where Eyvind used twelves. He tried to show them how to count on their fingers, joint by joint, with the pointing thumb: one two three, one two three, one two three, one two three. Twelve. They found this hilarious, flashing their ten fingers at him, then insisting that he show his hands to them to see if he had any additional fingers. He would give up and wander off to look at horses again.

He saw mares being milked. He saw individual animals caught with rope and pole and taken off to work or slaughter. Mostly he watched the natural interactions of horses in groups: playing, grooming, grazing, fighting, sleeping. Anxious, patrolling stallions; submissive, playful geldings; wise old mares. Freakish little foals. Always he kept an eye out for the white horse as he scanned a constant sea of tossing brown and black manes. Often he thought he saw one in the middle distance, but he could never approach it. Sometimes he would see a flash of white, but it would just turn out to be a horse with a blaze or a star or a white leg. He asked the herders. They told him that they had no white horses. They were always rare among the local breed, and right now there were none. Of this they were certain. Such horses, they said, were especially prized as sacrifices. Nonetheless, Eyvind felt sure that he saw one. He even tried to point it out to them—a white shape on a distant hill, white ears and a muzzle briefly thrown upward in a crowd of heads, the whisk of a white tail vanishing behind a row of brown backs. None of them ever saw it.

On the morning of the fiftieth day, when all remained quiet in the *qan*'s camp, Eyvind was summoned to the large tent. He was given ten horses and the gift of choosing them from the herd. He was awarded an honoured place at the rear of the tent, such as no foreigner had ever been given before. His ownership of the concubine, the boy, and the old woman was confirmed. Hoë'lün was present and she seemed very pleased. She, too, was given ten horses. Eyvind was impressed at how much the *qan* was willing to spend in gratitude. He thanked the *qan* and his magicians with appropriate ceremony. Eyvind was highly satisfied with this outcome. He was going to be able to return home with twenty-five horses and a load of *isgeir*. Even with losses on the journey, this cargo would be worth an enormous sum in Iceland. He was on his way to becoming a rich man.

When he returned to his tent, the white horse was waiting by the door. It was calm. She was calm; he saw now that the horse was a mare. She stood quietly, swishing her tail. Her dark eyes were peaceable. Eyvind touched her neck. She considered him mildly.

Eyvind was appalled. It was apparent to him that he had saved the *qan*'s people from further trouble only to end up with a personal haunting. He felt sure that Hoë'lün had expected something of this kind and was filled with fury. He stalked away to find the mother of Bortë. The horse did not follow but remained by the door, not grazing, merely waiting with one hip cocked, resting a hind leg. Eyvind wondered if she were lame. Could ghost horses go lame?

He found Hoë'lün in her tent. She did not look surprised to see him. "Come with me," Eyvind said. Hoë'lün followed him to his own tent without protest. "Do you see that horse?" he demanded. The horse was hard to miss. Hoë'lün looked past it. Past her.

Hoë'lün looked at him with pity. "Foreigner," she said, "you have done us a great service, so for this one time I will speak frankly. This horse that you imagine yourself to see, standing here, is unnatural. If she were here, she would be a flesh and blood animal, able to carry riders and bear foals. If she were here, she would be a fine investment. If such an animal were to exist, she would be a wind horse: a human soul, now in a horse's flesh."

"A troll!" interrupted Eyvind.

Hoë'lün continued as if he had not spoken. "Such an animal is impossible. If it should ever happen to exist, it would doubtless have remarkable powers. In the event that such a horse were ever discovered here, we would be required to sacrifice it. Fortunately, I myself, and the tribal magicians, have confirmed to the *qan* and his people that no such animal could ever be found here. For as you know, and the herders have confirmed, this is a tribe with no white horses. You will therefore find that, regardless of whatever you imagine yourself to be seeing, nobody will be prepared to accept its being there."

Eyvind could see that he had been thoroughly trapped. On the other hand, he had a free horse. She was a fine specimen. "Does this horse pose any danger to me?" he asked her.

"Such a horse would not," replied Hoë'lün. "Such a horse, having the vestige of a human being inside her—a soul, for example, such as the one that belonged to my daughter Bortë—would possess unusual intelligence, resourcefulness, and luck. These qualities would, in most circumstances, communicate themselves to whomever was the master of such a horse."

"This mare is Bortë?" asked Eyvind.

Hoë'lün looked horrified. "Horses have no names! This white mare, should she happen to exist, could not possibly have a name! Bortë was the name of my daughter, who is dead. Do you understand?"

"Yes," said Eyvind. "The mare has no name."

Hoë'lün looked calmer. "Wind of the island, let me tell you one more thing. You do not want to hear this thing. Nonetheless, I tell it to you. You are a magician. Not a great one, for nobody knows your bloodline, but you have some power. Magician to magician, I may be able to help you with a problem that you have. I am willing to do so because you have done me a great favour."

"What is this problem?" said Eyvind.

"Sterility," replied Hoë'lün.

Eyvind was ashamed. "Why do you say such a thing?" he asked.

"It is not uncommon among male magicians," said

Hoë'lün, with a trace of smugness. "Their manhood may be compromised by their profession. Also, your concubine is as fertile as a marmot and is not pregnant. She has borne three children to three different men."

"I have never wanted to be a magician. I despise *seithr*," said Eyvind. "I will accept your help."

"There is only a small chance of it working," warned Hoë'lün. "But I owe you."

"Fine," said Eyvind. "What do we do?"

"First of all, we should do it far from here," said Hoë'lün. "Men will understand what I am doing when they see it. You will not wish to be shamed before men who know you. I suggest we go to my camp where you are unknown. We will tell the *qan* that you are going there to witness a final libation that must be poured on the fiftieth day on the ground of the magician who performed the ritual."

Eyvind was impressed at the magician's canniness. Nor did he wish to be shamed before David or the *qan*. He agreed. Giving the *qan* this excuse, they departed right away. Hoë'lün drove a felt-covered cart. She tied the senior mare of the group of horses she had chosen as gifts to it. The other horses followed her reluctantly. They set off for Hoë'lün's camp. Looking back, Eyvind saw the white mare following with the others.

Hoë'lün owed allegiance to the neighbouring chieftain. He had a tentative alliance with the *qan* known to Eyvind, and so for the moment did not call himself *qan*. When Hoë'lün arrived home, she poured a libation before her own tent, as she had said that she would. Then, as it was night, she retired inside and Eyvind came with her. Her tent was spacious and she was well supplied with goods and servants, so Eyvind was comfortable. "We will conduct the ritual at dawn," she said.

The next morning Hoë'lün gave him milk to drink but no other food. She called to her two senior herdsmen. Together, all four of them approached the camp's herd. Hoë'lün picked out a young animal that she owned, a stud colt of nearly two years. "That one," she said. The two men caught it with rope and pole. This took a long time. Eyvind was by this time quite hungry, but knew better than to complain. "Geld it," said Hoë'lün. The two men threw the horse down in a skilled fashion, tied one of its hind legs to its forelegs, and gelded it with a sharp knife. The horse, stunned, did not scream or thrash. As soon as they removed the cords binding its leg, it was on its feet again. One of the herders cut a short section of cord and tied one testicle to the horse's tail. Then he released the horse, and it bolted off, the testicle dragging and bouncing behind it. The other he was about to place in a bag at his waist, but Hoë'lün said, "Give it to me." The herdsman at once handed it over. Both of the men looked at each other and then at Eyvind. Eyvind could sense a joke in the air but could do nothing about it. He turned and followed Hoë'lün, who was already walking away.

"Why did he tie the testicle to the tail?" asked Eyvind.

Hoë'lün looked at him in some surprise. "By the time it has dried the wound will be healed," she replied. "Do you not do that in your herds at home?"

"I have never heard of it," said Eyvind. "It is a good trick. As to the other, I expect I will have to eat it?"

"Exactly," said Hoë'lün.

"Cooked?" said Eyvind.

"No," said Hoë'lün.

Eyvind was unsurprised. Magic was not about comfort but symmetry. If his balls were cooked, this task was about making them raw again.

He followed Hoë'lün into her tent. She dismissed her cook and other servants and skinned and sliced the testicle very thinly with her own hands. She spoke some words and sprinkled some herbs on the slices, which she served on a plate made of red clay. Eyvind ate them without fuss. Then she broke the plate.

"Is that all?" asked Eyvind.

"Yes, the unlocking is done," replied Hoë'lün. "It is a simple magic, but there is some chance it will be effective."

"How will I know?"

"If you have a child," Hoë'lün said.

"I will thank you on that day," said Eyvind, "but it seems to me unlikely. Both that you could identify this sickness or cure it."

"Both are unlikely. Yet you came," said Hoë'lün. "Living is an unlikely business. You are a man who does unlikely things. Why else would you be here, so far from home? Why would you act on behalf of my daughter, a woman not your wife or kin, whose language you can but barely understand? A woman no longer even alive? Most men would not travel so far as a pregnant woman goes to piss for such a person. It may be that you crossed the world for her. I cannot say. It is unlikely."

"Do you really think I am a magician?" asked Eyvind.

"I think you can listen with both ears," said Hoë'lün.

———

Not long after this, Eyvind and David and their party were ready to depart from the *qan*'s camp. They had with them seventy-five horses, fifty packed or harnessed to wagons of goods and twenty-five free with two herdsmen. Eyvind had opted to invest all his money that had not gone into the fifteen horses he had bought in a cargo of *isgeir*. He felt sure it would be well received in Iceland, and that, having taken care to observe its production, he could profit in advising people how to make it. Here it was often made from the hair of long-haired cattle or *tebe* in addition to wool, but there was no reason why it could not be made exclusively of sheep's wool. It was a marvellous fabric, utterly waterproof and windproof if correctly treated, and took nothing to make but some reed or wood frames, being simply crushed together. In the *qan*'s country rolls of wet *isgeir*, wrapped in hides, were pulled by two horses, usually at great speed. Young men did this at the gallop, pulling the rolls along between them, turning on a long axle like a great wheel. The process was very dramatic; Eyvind could imagine young men doing so in Iceland. But the rolling and pressing could also be done in less dramatic ways. Distaffs need have nothing to do with this cloth-making, he thought with some bitterness. Though of course such an important activity could not be conducted without invocations and libations, so an *udugan* or other magician was always involved.

The horses, of course—twenty-six in total, including his gifts from the *qan* and the mare with no name, though he was not certain whether he should reckon her an asset—were wealth unimaginable. The horses native to the *qan*'s country were exactly the kind to thrive in the rocky ice and fire of Iceland, if he could only get them there, all the way overland and then by river-boat and then by ship over the ocean. They were small, hairy, and tough. They needed no shoes. They lived wild in low temperatures and found their own food, even in snow. They were the horses of heroes, thought Eyvind. Or at least, the horses of heroes who aspired, in the end, to be farmers in a land far from any king, no matter how harsh that land was.

Eyvind departed the *qan*'s country without either of his female slaves. Women are a bone of contention on a long journey. He asked both of the women their preference, and they both said they would like to remain. He gave the old woman to Hoë'lün. He had seen that her tent was comfortable and life there untroubled. Hoë'lün said that she would keep her for as long as she could be said to do any work. If she did not die in the tent as a worker she would be exposed. This had always been her fate. Eyvind was well acquainted with the extent to which what Hoë'lün said became what was. The old woman would live a long life. The concubine he returned to the *qan*'s tent with compliments and commendation. There was a man there in the *qan*'s service, father of her third child, whom she loved and to whom she wanted to return. As she had borne no child to Eyvind, this was easily arranged. So he left them in what comfort he could, seeking no profit from them, as he had made so much already. He took only the boy with him. The child was an orphan from a subject tribe, most of whom had been exterminated. As long as Eyvind had known him he had been called Jat, but when he set out on the journey away from the steppes of his birth he begged to be called Geirr. Eyvind, pleased with this streak of imagination and independence, agreed to do so.

David had a more diverse cargo than Eyvind. So did most of his men. Most of them had made the journey before. They knew what to buy and how to dispose of it on the way back. None of them had as far to go as Eyvind. Some planned to remain in Khazaria and some to follow David all the way back to Helmgard. They all knew that they were now facing the most dangerous part of their trip: travelling across a great distance of land recently devastated by war, transporting valuable cargo and a sizeable herd of horses. Horses are worth good money everywhere, and everybody wants them. The Khazars wanted to sell their horses to their countrymen in Khazaria to help their king recoup his losses against the Rus and the Greeks—which they had heard had been considerable, though reports were vague at such a distance. They did not want them looted by desperate men or strangers. Eyvind wanted to pass clear through their territory keeping as many horses as he possibly could. So everyone was heavily armed and nervous as they set out.

Eyvind had to deal with the curious question of how to treat the mare with no name. Should he treat her as a riding horse? Would such an animal permit this? Or should he keep her unbroken, running free with the herd? As far as he could see, she behaved like a normal horse. None of the other horses treated her as uncanny, and she had found her rank within the group. David's men thought her unusual in being white, but that was all. Whatever they had heard or speculated about concerning her origins they kept to themselves. David was particularly silent on this question. Only the people of the *qan* had treated her as invisible, and now they were almost out of his territory. Eyvind decided that the only thing to do was put it to the test. He had ridden women before, so there was no point being overly punctilious.

Adopting the straightforward method of the *qan*'s herdsmen, he singled out the mare from the herd with rope and pole, and with the help of one of the Khazars, bridled and saddled her and jumped on. The second man let go and she squealed and bolted immediately, scattering the herd. Eyvind hung on grimly and let her run herself out. She was young and strong, so this took a long time. Both were exhausted by the time she came to a stop several hours later. Eyvind, however, was still on her back. Therefore, he had won. The mare understood this and accepted his directions by rein and leg. This was the simple foundation of all the great horsemanship he had seen on the steppes. The *qan*'s men and their horses trained for war, yes. But really, the horses were half-wild. They went for weeks or months without being ridden or harnessed. They were caught and tamed each time by this method. Power relations were thus absolutely clear. A man mounted on a horse dominated it. A man not mounted on a horse left it alone to look after itself. So Eyvind established that the white mare was a rideable horse.

They went on for many weeks without meeting anybody. The Khazars grew steadily more anxious. They were within days of the outlying villages on the eastern border. They ought to have met local traders and shepherds by now. Such silence was bad. It spoke of desperation. When they arrived at the first village they learned a lot. Upon seeing the smoke rising from the chimneys, and seeing house walls and corrals standing and crops unburnt, both David and Benjamin muttered to themselves something that Eyvind assumed was a prayer of thanks to their deity. They proceeded into the main street of the village, their baggage train taking up most of it. The loose horses they left outside of the croplands with their two herders. Both were armed with bows. David, Benjamin, and one other went to the house of the village headman. They invited Eyvind to come with them, though merely out of politeness as he did not speak the language. Still, due to the gifts Eyvind had received from the *qan*, he owned more horses than any of them. His stake in the enterprise was considerable. Thus he went with them.

The headman had a lot to say. David translated some of it, but clearly not all. Meanwhile, Eyvind enjoyed sitting on a chair at a table in a house with firm walls. He drank some kind of tasty herbal drink that was brewed hot. Everything inside the headman's house, though it was small, seemed strangely bright and far away. There was a hearth with a shiny round kettle hanging above the fire. After a while the headman's wife, who wore a kerchief over her hair, brought out what was unmistakably bread, three broad flat loaves like shield bosses. The traders looked at them reverently. When they were invited to do so, they ate them quickly, without speaking, then thanked their hosts. David looked at Eyvind with amusement and said, "Our old friend the *qan* speaks slightingly of people who live behind walls, but it is usually behind walls that you find bread." Eyvind nodded fervently, chewing. It struck him for the first time that of the wheat flour they had brought to the *qan*'s court, he had seen nothing the whole time he had been there. It was obviously hoarded or kept only for the *qan*'s private use.

"There are no walls thick enough to keep out our present calamity," said the headman, "or, not for long. All that has kept us alive over here is the barrier of the Itil." The conversation turned serious then. He told them that Alp Tarkhan had barely survived the summer assault of the Rus and their unreliable Greek allies, with whom they had fallen out partway through the campaign. This disagreement, though it could be considered fortunate, had caused even greater destruction in the region, as the enemies had split into two competing armies that fought with each other as well as the Khazars. The Tarkhan had been wounded and lost thousands of men and horses. Nonetheless, he had stopped both armies getting to the river and destroying the sacred city of Itil. Both David and Benjamin muttered their prayer again. The unfinished fortification at Sarkel had been overrun and dug up and hundreds of leagues around it devastated, as the foreign armies had dwelt there for months, looting and fighting among themselves before burning everything behind them as they left in two directions.

"What of the *bäk*?" asked David.

"We have heard nothing of the *bäk* and are filled with terror. News is slow crossing the river. We have heard little of the capital except that it still stands. Khwarezmians guard it. Alp Tarkhan is rebuilding Sarkel. Some people think this is unlucky, but he is doing it anyway. He is rebuilding the army, as well." The headman added, "He will need horses."

David and Benjamin looked at each other. "If the Khwarezmians are guarding the city, then the *bäk* still has silver to pay them," said Benjamin.

"Perhaps he does," said David, "but they are foreigners. He will expect more of his own people."

"Well, he can expect nothing of me," said Eyvind. "I bought these horses for Icelanders, not to be lost in the wars of Khazaria."

"I do my work to make a profit," said David. "Yet I will not see my country overrun by the Rus, either. I hope to find a middle ground."

"You can hope that," said the headman. "If that is what you hope, hire more guards."

Eyvind approved of this idea. Considering the wealth they were carrying, they seemed to him to be undermanned. The villagers had their crops planted, by the looks of things. Some might come as caravan guards. A fighting man is more useful if he speaks the local language. The Khazars spoke among themselves about this at some length. The headman said he could spare five men. They negotiated some more. At length all agreed. Five villagers with their own arms and horses would attend on them at least as far as Sarkel, so long as their wages were paid. They would help to guard the baggage and horses. They went out to inform the other men of this good news.

Eyvind would have preferred simply to get to the river and head back along it towards Aldeigjuborg and Helmgard, north and then west into the lands of the Rus. This, he thought, had been David's original plan. Things were now different. The Khazars could not now be certain that they would be well received at the river ports once they were within Garthariki. If they were not stopped or killed, and their goods confiscated, tolls would be exorbitantly high. They were now of the opinion that they should cross the river and make towards Sarkel until they met with agents of Alp Tarkhan, where they could at least dispose of their horses at a marginal profit. Eyvind was wary of this idea, as he did not want his precious horses devoured by the Tarkhan's war. Khazar politics were no concern of his. On the other hand, Khazars spoke a difficult language and controlled the ports on the lower Itil. They would also consider Eyvind to be Rus. The fact that he did not consider himself so would not concern them. Eyvind doubted that he could get a valuable and unwieldy cargo through those river ports without David's help. It was a frustrating situation. Such safety as there was lay in numbers. He decided to stay with David's party. He only did so, however, after securing from David a promise to accompany him through the Khazar-controlled stretch of the river afterwards. Whether any of the Khazar traders would proceed further upriver into the Rus lands was not yet known. It was the best Eyvind could do.

The party, enlarged by its new guards, set off towards the Itil. It was now perhaps a week away. The land was not populous. The main territory of Khazaria was on the other side of the river. These were only a few towns and villages that straggled over that boundary. What linked these people to the empire was mostly the language, which was separate from that spoken by other tribes nearby such as the Bulghurs or, further east, the people of the *qan*. Few of these villagers spoke the river-language that was used at the upper end of the river that the Rus controlled. Only wide-travelling traders like David's men did so. They usually used this language when speaking with Eyvind. Now, Eyvind noticed, they were reluctant to do so, or to speak to him at all. The news about the Rus war had angered them. This made him uneasy.

They reached the bank of the Itil, strong with spring floodwaters. They proceeded along it until they came to a tiny village, only a few houses and a dock. Forewarned by one of their villager-guards, the headman had mustered some flat-bottomed boats, and these they used to ferry the horses across the river. Getting seventy-five near-wild horses across was a painful task. Three men were injured. The headman asked a steep price but knocked it back a fraction when told sternly by Benjamin that the horses were on their way to the army of Alp Tarkhan.

Then they were in Khazaria. They packed up and organized their train and the free horses with their herdsmen. As they worked, for the first time, Eyvind heard the Khazars sing all together, a song in their own language. Hitherto they had sung little, and often only fragments of scurrilous songs in the river-language, perhaps out of deference to Eyvind. Now they sang a long and complicated song of which Eyvind understood not a word. Of David's language he knew only *ät* and *tebe* and a few common words for utensils and horse's tack. It was an impressive language with strong sounds, but Eyvind could not see into it. That was the way it was with languages, Eyvind had observed once he left home and realized how many there were: some he could see into and some he could not. Listening to them was like looking down into a stream. Sometimes the water was muddy and sometimes clear. Hearing their song, Eyvind understood that the wind of their home country was acting upon the Khazars.

They rode across a rolling but not steep country sectioned by streams. There were more trees than Eyvind had seen for some time. The grass was level and short and very green, with little sign of old growth in it. "Fire," said David tersely, looking around at it. Everyone was quiet. For days they rode and saw no-one, only birds and small animals in the grass. No herds, not even deer. The men became grimmer and spoke to Eyvind less and less. Then they began to pass burnt homesteads and farms, just fragments of blackened timber and scorched stone walls. Eyvind thought as he rode on that a considerable number of folk must have lived in this region. Finally, many days into Khazaria, they came to a farmhouse that was still standing. David and Benjamin and a few more men went in. They searched all around to see if anyone was still living, but soon they declared it empty.

They decided to spend the night there. It was shelter. There was a hearth and an unblocked chimney. They were crowded, but many men had to stay outside to watch over the horses so it was manageable. Eyvind stayed outside as a horse guard. He did not feel comfortable among the glowering men. To his surprise the white mare came to him and lipped his hair affectionately, as one horse will do to another. She stayed with him by his fire at one edge of the herd, which was ringed with men and fires, appearing to enjoy its warmth. Then, also to his surprise, David appeared, looking bleak. He nodded to the white mare as if to a business companion, and said to Eyvind, "Look here." He handed him a weighty gold coin.

Eyvind recognized it as a dirham. "From Sarkland?" he said. "Did you just find it? Well, I suppose one coin counts as a hoard."

"Not from Sarkland. From Khazaria. Only a few like

this were ever minted," replied David, looking strained. He took the coin back, and showed Eyvind its glinting edge in the firelight. It was ringed with words but Eyvind could not read them. "That word there, that is the name Moses, a Hebrew patriarch. These coins date from the time of Manasseh, father of our *bäk*. They are few and precious, above and beyond the gold they contain, especially prized by men who share the royal faith. Probably there were Jews here. They are dead now along with everybody else. I found it just inside the threshold of the house, and afterwards I found I could not bear to be inside. An enormous sorrow and dread rose inside me. Now I feel I might howl like a dog," said David. He put the coin in his pocket with trembling hands.

The mare, who had been standing there as if listening, nudged Eyvind. Eyvind looked at her and then at the distressed merchant, wondering if this gesture was significant or trivial. David had not noticed. He was staring into the fire.

"You and Benjamin, both, it seems to me, have uttered blessings and prayers in my hearing," said Eyvind. "Have you no prayer or invocation you might say for the dead?"

"Yes," said David. "I could speak an ancient praise poem, but there must be nine Jewish men with me."

"Or your god will not hear you? He requires compurgation? He is a stickler, your god," said Eyvind.

"As I did not make this rule, I cannot break it," replied David.

"Have you no other options?" asked Eyvind. "What do people say at a burial?"

"There is a prayer, true, for a funeral, at the time when a tithe is paid towards a charitable cause," replied David, thoughtfully, "though the name of the deceased is supposed to be uttered within it. I am not certain it would be valid."

"About that I cannot advise you," said Eyvind. "But if you bury this coin with the name of Moses and say these words over it with great conviction, in the name of Jews who have died in Khazaria, perhaps it will suffice. After all, you will have both a funeral and a donation."

"This is not a matter for joking," said David.

"I did not joke," said Eyvind. "It is what I would do if I felt a similar compulsion. That is all."

"You are an innovator," said David, disapprovingly.

"I suppose I am," said Eyvind. "Circumstances keep changing." The mare nudged him again. This time David noticed. He gazed at the white horse for a long time. Then, nodding farewell to Eyvind, he departed.

"I don't think he wanted your advice," Eyvind said to the mare. "There are no women priests in Judaism."

———

As they went on through Khazaria, the only ones who were happy were the horses. They were happy with the new grass. The men were grim. Eyvind pictured himself riding through Eyri and seeing only desolation. He kept that image firmly in mind on the occasion of his getting into a fight with a Khazar, Adal, who refused to serve him food one night at the cooking fire. *Yabanci*, said the man, and spat into the flames. This led to a fistfight, but one that remained private and did not escalate. It is unwise to let yourself be subject to insult, but at the same time it is unwise for a man who is being singled out to act disproportionately. Eyvind knocked the man down and walked away. No-one took up Adal's cause, though there was some muttering. Eyvind appealed to Benjamin, who had seen everything, and both men went to David and laid the matter before him as chief of the party. David ruled that Adal owed Eyvind an ell of *isgeir*. There the matter rested. Eyvind observed thereafter that there were some members of the party who looked at David and Benjamin with harder eyes than before. Both Jews were well aware of this.

They were drawing near Sarkel, and all the men were now looking out for outriders of the army of the Tarkhan. But instead of finding the Tarkhan's soldiers, they were found by them, and Eyvind learned that the *qan*'s folk were not the only good soldiers in this part of the world.

One morning they awoke surrounded by thirty-five armed men. Eyvind was impressed that not only had they managed to get close to them with so little cover, but that scouts must have informed them of their exact number, such that they had sent enough men to subdue them under normal circumstances, and no more. This spoke of an intelligent commander.

David and Benjamin went out, unarmed, to talk with these men. Conversation immediately came around to the horses. The question was not whether the horses were going to become part of the Khazar army, but simply under what terms. Eyvind did not care about the profits or motives of David's men, but he did not want his horses sold. How he could accomplish this was not clear to him. Men representing the army of Khazaria were not likely to think much of the objections raised by a man they would identify as Rus. If they even noticed that he was there they were likely to kill him and confiscate both horses and cargo. He could not count on the caravan to defend him, with the Khazar traders in their present mood. So he skulked in the background of the negotiations. This galled him. He had already made his position clear to David, however, so he would have to trust him. This was a severe test.

It was a severe test that David failed. He was wholly unable to get Alp Tarkhan's men to make an exception for Eyvind's herd. They insisted on taking all the horses. They were prepared to pay for them, but that was all. It was clear that if David pressed too hard, they would just take the horses as a patriotic donation. There was nothing David could do. His men were outnumbered already and they were within a day's ride of the base at Sarkel, where there were hundreds of men still gathered. "I am sorry, Eyvind," he said, and made the best deal he could. The Icelander would get a certain number of dirhams out of it, but that was all. All seventy-five horses—including the mare with no name—were to be driven off at dawn to Sarkel. So things stood when an infuriated Eyvind wrapped himself in his blankets to sleep that night.

In the morning the Tarkhan's men paid over the money and drove off the herd of horses. As seven more men had arrived during the night, there was no possibility of the traders' objecting or trying to fight. The Khazars did not want to, anyway. Adal smirked at Eyvind, seeing his rage. Eyvind resigned himself to watching his investment gallop away. He wondered what the white mare would do. He had been unable to save her. She would die as the mount of a Khazar warrior in some battle with the Rus. He saw her on the farthest westward fringe of the herd, at what was about to become the leading edge of a stampede as their zealous new owners drove them towards the fortress. Soon enough there came a chorus of yips and whoops and the herd panicked and began to move. Horses neighed and snorted, calling out to each other. Eyvind heard one particularly loud, distinct cry.

Then he saw a remarkable thing. The white mare was not running with the others. She remained still as the others ran past her. And as the other members of the herd, rushing and panicking, came abreast of her, a few of them stopped. Others veered round them. One or two of each successive wave of horses stopped as they approached the line at which the white mare stood, as suddenly as if they had been reined in. Their herd mates flashed around them fluidly. For a moment in the flying mêlée a brief, triangular island of slowing horses formed, the others flowing around them on either side. Then the main herd was gone, racing across the grass, furlongs widening between it and a perfect line of horses, as straight as if a wall were set before them. The mare stood in the middle of this line. For a moment she stood alertly, looking back towards Eyvind. Then she began cropping grass, unconcerned. The other horses followed suit, breaking their formation, wandering and nibbling.

Twenty-one horses remained, including the mare. All of them belonged to Eyvind. Six of his gift horses from the *qan* had fled with the others. Four had stayed, along with all the horses he had bought and his roan gelding.

Eyvind stood dumbfounded, waiting for a hue and cry to begin when the Tarkhan's men realized that they had left horses behind. But the herd and the herders galloped away, never stopping. He turned back towards David's men, certain that some of them would call out after them, telling them to stop. For one thing, they would certainly fear reprisal if the army felt it had been cheated. But his fellow traders were turning away, grumbling about prices, moving gloomily towards the carts, complaining that they no longer had horses to pull them. Not one of them so much as looked back at the reduced herd. Eyvind gaped after them. His horses remained invisible to everyone but him.

As soon as Eyvind realized this he walked out to congratulate the mare on her achievement. He brought her a bit of salt, which she seemed to appreciate. What the other men thought he was doing wandering around in an empty field he did not trouble himself about. They were sufficiently distracted arguing about how to redistribute the baggage. These arguments, and much moving around of goods and agonizing about what would need to be left behind, occupied them well into the night. Eyvind, feeling that it was no more than they deserved, said nothing. For one thing, he had no idea when, or even if, the horses would return to visibility.

At dawn, an utterly astonished David woke him, saying that his horses had returned during the night. "I told you that my horses were not for sale," said Eyvind.

"God of Israel!" said David, as he watched the twenty-one horses milling about. "Do you think we should assign new herders?"

"I expect so," replied Eyvind. Two men were set to watch over the herd, as before. They seemed rather nervous about their task.

Everyone was aware that something uncanny had happened. All the Khazars looked at Eyvind askance and gave the white mare a wide berth. "But what about Alp Tarkhan?" asked one man, quite sensibly in Eyvind's opinion. "Won't he come after us?" Unfortunately, Eyvind had no answer for him. He did not know how far the mare's magic extended. He therefore advised that they pack up and head back towards the river immediately. All saw the wisdom of this. A great deal of uncanniness was forgiven Eyvind once they realized that they now had horses to pull their wagons. Eyvind magnanimously allowed his horses to cart other men's goods as they headed back towards the Itil.

As they rode through more ruinous country, Alp Tarkhan did not pursue them. The mare's magic held.

Gradually the Khazars relaxed. They had made more profit than expected and still had had the satisfaction of swelling the ranks of their imperial army. Eyvind took half the money that he was owed for his horses that the army had ostensibly bought, but permitted the other traders to divide the rest of the extra profit. Nobody saw fit to argue with this. Indeed, most thanked him for his generosity. Eyvind felt more secure knowing that they owed him. He knew he would need their help to pass along the river until they were out of Khazaria. Mind you, should any of them decide to go on to Aldeigjuborg or Helmgard, they might need him to act as spokesman for them. None of this would become clear until they had better news about the state of the river trade. Meanwhile, they were still bound together. The ill-feeling that Eyvind had sensed rising against him had been transformed into respect and fear now that he had been revealed to be a powerful magician.

Even David, intolerant of magic, had changed his attitude. "Something happened to you in the *qan*'s country," he said, "that I would never have expected of such a hard-headed man."

"True," said Eyvind.

"Was it that *udugan*, Hoë'lün? Did she put a spell on you?" he asked.

"I would prefer not to discuss it," said Eyvind.

"Quite so," replied David, looking at him with wonder,

"it would be irreligious of me to do so. I beg your pardon." But it was clear that he remained curious. Eyvind observed him staring at the white mare for long periods. Eyvind caught a number of Khazars staring at him the same way when they thought he would not notice. Magic cuts across all faiths.

As they were encamped one night, a lone horseman rode up to them. He was a brave man, Eyvind thought, to approach so many without hesitation. He did not dismount, or lay down his arms, or make any signs of truce or appeasement but rode straight up to the fire. His boots thumped on the ground as he dismounted. His horse was far taller than any in Eyvind's herd. It was certainly the tallest Eyvind had ever seen, long-legged and lean, with a coat that gleamed and reflected the firelight. The man was also tall and lean, made taller by a pale headdress that was wrapped about his head. Eyvind wondered if he were a Sark. He had only seen one or two before.

David and Benjamin rose and spoke to the man. He answered them fluently in their own language. They spoke for some time, and the man allowed another of the party to unsaddle his tall and beautiful horse. He hobbled it with his own hands and released it to graze within sight of the fire. Eyvind could not take his eyes off it. Even in the dark it was the most magnificent beast he had ever seen.

The man sat down among them with no sign of fear. Seated, he was taller than all of them except Eyvind, at whom he gazed questioningly across the flames. David spoke, saying, "This stranger is a man of Khwarazem, a member of the *bäk's* guard. He is named Ibrahim." The stranger nodded. "And this"—David gestured towards Eyvind—"is our fellow traveller, Eyvind, a man of Iceland." Eyvind nodded. Then Ibrahim and David and Benjamin spoke at length. The two Khazars looked more and more sober. Other men listening to them cried out and exclaimed. One wept, covering his eyes. Eyvind understood that they were hearing terrible news.

The man Ibrahim spoke with great sobriety and formality, as befit the news he was relating. Eyvind waited to hear what it was. Finally, David turned to him and said, his face pale, "Our *bäk* is dead. His priests spent many weeks preparing the burial site, altering a watercourse and damming it in preparation. The *bäk* yielded up his life"—here David made a slight hand gesture, so quick that Eyvind's eye could not follow it—"and was buried beneath it immediately, according to the rite. Now water flows over him." He made the gesture again, a flick of the hand.

"His people sacrificed him?" asked Eyvind. "For the failure of the war? Who now is *bäk*, then?"

"Ibrahim told us that the king-tribes were still in debate a month ago when he departed the city. He has since been to Sarkel, whence he followed us."

"Has he come about the horses?" asked Eyvind.

"No," replied David. "That is not his concern. He has said nothing about it. He came to bring us news of this great and holy event. And he heard that we had mare's butter among our trade goods. He has come to purchase some."

"He came all this way for butter?" said Eyvind.

"So it would seem," said David. He turned back to Ibrahim with more questions. Other traders likewise posed them. Eyvind did not recognize any words they were saying, so they were unlikely to concern trade goods. He supposed them to relate to this important royal ritual. He let them talk and gazed at the traveller's horse. Eventually they all went to bed. The stranger was given a place in the best tent.

In the early morning Eyvind went out to piss and spotted the man unrolling a small rug and crouching upon it and performing some kind of ritual. He pretended not to see. People often preferred that their rituals not be observed. Ibrahim paid no attention and carried on with his task, whatever it was.

Later, as they broke their fast around the fire, Eyvind observed Ibrahim asking a series of questions of David and Benjamin as they ate. He seemed keenly interested in the answers. Both of the Khazars looked uncomfortable and spoke stiffly. Eyvind wondered what they could be talking about. It appeared to be of some importance. After a while the tall and bearded man looked over at Eyvind, and asked them another question. David laughed sourly and said to Eyvind, "He is asking if you are a Christian. I told him you were not."

"Why would he want to know that?"

"Because then, if you chanced to be the one who prepared the food, he could eat it. As he can if I do, or Benjamin does. We are people of the book, as he is."

"What do books have to do with food?" Eyvind would eat any food that a host gave him, provided that it was not poisoned. This was the only sane way of proceeding. Food was hard to come by, usually.

"He is a follower of the prophet Mohammed and his religion has many laws concerning food, as does Judaism. They are, in fact, most stringent."

"Do you observe these rules?" asked Eyvind.

"As best I can, in the circumstances," David replied.

"Is that what you were talking to him about before?" asked Eyvind, curiously. "These rules? He ate the food, I notice. Who prepared it?"

"I did," said David.

"How fortunate," said Eyvind. "What if I had?"

David looked at him severely. "You are a pagan. He would not have eaten it."

Ibrahim looked inquiringly over at them. David spoke to him and they had a brief exchange. "He says that he might if it were a matter of necessity," said David.

"He sounds like a lawyer," said Eyvind.

David translated this and the man grinned. He looked at Eyvind and said something. David went on, "And he says further that all of the people of the book must be lawyers at heart."

"So are Icelanders," said Eyvind. "In fact, so are the people of the *qan*. Their life is full of laws."

"But not books," said David.

Eyvind suddenly thought of something. "They had one book," he said. "Though they don't have it any longer. Hoë'lün gave it to me."

"What are you talking about?" asked David.

Eyvind rose and went to search in his wagon. After a time he returned with a roll of calfskin about two hands' breadth. It was tied with a thong. Untied, it fell to a length of half an ell or so. It was a fine skin, well cured and scraped. It was covered with writing. Eyvind showed it to them proudly. He had scarcely thought about it before. Ibrahim was interested and rose to see it. He gestured politely to see if he might hold it. Eyvind gave it to him. David and several other men stood nearby, all looking at it.

"Do you know what it is?" asked David.

"Hoë'lün said that it was the story of her daughter

Bortë's ghost," replied Eyvind. "She spoke it to a scribe who was visiting their chieftain. She said she was most impressed watching him write it, how the shapes grew like trees. She could not read it herself, and nor can I. But she said that I should take it, as it pertains in a certain way to my white mare."

Ibrahim considered the document, turning it various ways in his hands. He said something to David, looking puzzled. "It is no writing that he can recognize," explained David, "neither Persian nor Arabic nor the script used by Christian traders. He wonders if it might be Khitan. They write in such columns."

"It is not Hebrew or Greek," said David, conferring with Benjamin.

"All I know is that the *qan*'s folk do not write things down. The man who wrote it was a foreigner," said Eyvind, "and Hoë'lün gave it to me, saying that it was her daughter's fate to be mixed up with foreign magic."

A man looking over Ibrahim's shoulder said, "It is Uighur. The writing."

Ibrahim handed the writing to him. He pored over it for some time, confused. "The script is Uighur; I know it from my grandmother. But this is not her language. The sounds recorded here do not make Uighur words." He began to make slow sounds, reading haltingly from the vellum, moving his finger. People tried to make sense of them, but they sounded like the words of a toddler.

"You know," said Benjamin after a while, "those might be words in the language of the *qan*'s country. *Daughter. Ghost. Fire.*"

"Well, it was Hoë'lün who spoke the words," said Eyvind. Not being a literate man, he felt less mystery than many of them. The man who knew the Uighur script was especially perturbed. "It makes no sense," he kept repeating.

"Look," said Eyvind, "what is the difficulty? Hoë'lün spoke the words in her language, and the man wrote them using these signs. They were the ones he knew. So that is the magic they enacted between them. We just have to eke the sounds back out of the skin."

"That is the magic of reading, yes," said David, sounding superior.

"There, then," said Eyvind. "It cannot be that remarkable." He rolled the vellum back up. He saw the eyes of Ibrahim watching him intently. It seemed the man had something to say. He spoke some words to David and Benjamin, spreading out his hands eloquently.

Benjamin said, addressing Eyvind, "On the contrary, it might be that what you hold is very remarkable. You may hold in your hands the only written words ever recorded in the *qan*'s language. Certainly such writings will be very few. Yours could be unique. That would make it very precious."

"Precious to whom?" said Eyvind. He was sceptical.

"Scholars. Priests. Men interested in the history of tongues," said David.

"Magicians," said Eyvind. "Or people who need to control ghosts."

The Khwarezmian looked very serious. He spoke and David translated: "Do not lose it. The written word is a key to many doors." Eyvind nodded and stowed the calf-skin roll carefully away among his other goods. He was surprised at the interest it had elicited. Among people he knew, things written down were usually tallies. On grave markers or rune stones, they were genealogies. True respect was reserved for words spoken aloud, in oaths or in poems. Significant men could muster a poem for any occasion. He himself had never been good at it. But then, he was not significant.

He returned to the foreigner. "Tell me about your horse," he said.

The horse, a bright bay mare, was called Gulab. She was nearly twice as tall at the withers as Eyvind's horses, smooth-coated, with long legs, flared nostrils, a dish face, and a rounded croup. At a trot she seemed to float above the ground. Ibrahim was exceedingly proud of her. He might have been her father, speaking her praise, or her servant, looking after her like a high-born lady. The Khazars found this comical. They knew such horses, bred in Sarkland. Eyvind did not. He found himself in agreement with Ibrahim about the merits of Gulab.

"That's not a horse but a courtesan," said David dismissively, well out of earshot of Ibrahim. "Do not offer to buy her. Remember, you are returning to Iceland. You would have to keep that horse in your bed. She needs blankets in winter. Special food. Shoes. They keep their horses indoors in Khwarazem, even in summer, each one in its own room."

What finally decided Eyvind against making a foolish offer for the magnificent mare was learning about the butter. Ibrahim had followed the traders' caravan for days and days in order to buy mare's butter to rub on his horse's legs. Not every day, he said, but after strain or heavy work, to prevent injury. Mare's butter was a much sought-after remedy, especially valued once it had gone rancid. *Boudra*, he called it. He had come all this way to buy as many vessels as he and the mare could carry. Buttering a live horse's leg seemed like the height of folly to Eyvind, and allowing good butter to go rancid for such a purpose was beyond understanding. Contemplating such waste brought his thoughts sharply back down to earth. He stood at the edge of the camp watching his own small, tough, rough-coated horses grazing. He looked at the mare with no name. She raised her head and looked back at him. He forgot Gulab.

Ibrahim accompanied them back to the river. He was a useful sort of man, a great rider and hunter. He told them all the news he had gleaned about the capital, though he was not greatly informed about the nobles' or merchants' quarters. Most of his time had been spent on the island in the sacred precinct of the king. Most of the Khazars scarcely dared ask about it. None had been to the island, or even dreamed of going there. Eyvind thought it was curious that a foreigner knew so much more about their holy of holies than they did. It occurred to him that access to power often resided with unexpected, even unwelcome people. He thought of the mad old woman in Eyri who practiced *seithr*, with her mumbling voice and cat skin gloves. Nobody wanted her company except in a crisis that could not be solved any other way. Anyone with wits would prefer, however, that she was interposed between himself, or herself, and Odin. If gods must be dealt with at all, who wants to do so directly?

Ibrahim was also a fine speaker of poetry. He did not do so in a language that Eyvind understood, which was too bad. Still, Eyvind knew a poet when he heard one. Words flowed out of him smoothly, and yet they were full of knots and recursions, patterns he could just discern even if he did not know what they meant. Other men who listened understood better, especially Benjamin, who had traded in Sarkland. Ibrahim, though he was Persian, spoke in Arabic, and the forms that he liked were Arabic forms. Benjamin did his best to translate one into the river-language.

At home in foreign lands I am not lost this night.
Night journeys are true though plains are not crossed this
night.

True home is absolute and high and everywhere,
A green oasis I could not exhaust this night.

Deserts are in the mind. There men may dry and parch,
Belovèd horses die, their manes wind-tossed, this night—

This night that is not now. A true night without love,
Prophets, law, saints, the whole graceful roster, this night.

Night calls to night, as day to day, and we in faith
Are stretched between, dashing for the postern this night.

Refuge is wider than the sky yet hard to find.
Who has taken Ibrahim to foster this night?

"I can't tell if that poem is about his god or his horse, or some woman," said Eyvind. "But there is no doubt it is impressive. It rolls like a wave."

Ibrahim left them at the Itil, riding off with Gulab wreathed about with wrapped pots of mare's butter. The traders rode into a port town, larger in scale than the mean village they had encountered downriver. The poor of this town looked thin and ragged and there was less in the market than there might have been, but trade was going forward. Those who wanted it secured passage towards Garthariki without trouble. Eyvind stayed out of the deal. He wore a hat to cover his light hair and kept near his horses. He let David take care of negotiations. Ten of David's men were travelling on northwards. The rest stayed behind, preferring to remain in Khazaria. Some sold on their goods to their compatriots heading towards the lands of the Rus, or gave them in consignment. Some stayed in the town to sell in the market there. Eyvind did not blame them. It was a risk for them to move on. Still, river-traders had told them that tolls upriver were high but that violence was not being offered towards foreign merchants. "Come to that, it's probably Greeks they'd be stopping, from what we've heard," said David.

The horses hated boarding the boat, the mare no less

than any of them. Nonetheless, they were shoved on. Eyvind looked at their fat, glossy sides ruefully. David had told him that shipmasters would insist that he starve his animals so they did not shit everywhere. He did not like to think of the walking skeletons his horses would be by the time they reached Iceland. David was right, and it did not make Eyvind happy, though it spared him costs in fodder. He would cheerfully have thrown half the passengers overboard to make room for the horses. But as it was not his ship, he could do nothing about it.

The long river passage was interminable. It seemed much longer than it had been coming downriver so many months ago, chiefly because Eyvind now had valuable cargo to worry about. With every day the horses got thinner and thinner. He feared he might lose his two stud colts, who were only yearlings, and gave them a bit of extra food. The white mare was dispirited but seemed healthy. He hoped that she would forgive him for the journey.

Three things enlivened this grim passage. Or perhaps one thing, in three aspects. All of them centred on the writing that the *udugan* had given Eyvind. The man who could read the Uighur script had come along on the voyage. So had Geirr, Eyvind's boy from the country of the *qan*. It transpired also that among the few additional passengers was a Greek priest. The man, Athanasios, was highly nervous. This was not a good time for a Greek to be travelling into Garthariki. Nonetheless, he said he had been called to a newly founded church in Helmgard. Eyvind assumed this was the work of Oleg, or more likely, Olga. The priest only knew the name of another priest, Simeon, who was already there. Though Athanasios spoke brashly of martyrdom, which Eyvind gathered was some kind of painful sacrifice, and claimed absolute faith in his deity's protection, he nonetheless hid himself in every port. Cowering there among the horses one day, he met with Geirr, who spent most of his time with the horses. Somehow the two struck up a conversation. Not long thereafter Geirr asked Eyvind to show the story of Bortë to the priest. Eyvind, who had nothing to occupy him, was willing to do so.

The priest, a learned man, was confounded. Eyvind was amused at his shock; he didn't much like the man. "This cannot be real writing!" Athanasios exclaimed at first. "It is the work of children, or perhaps of demons." Eyvind brought Ćimbai, the man whose grandmother had been an Uighur, to the priest. Ćimbai went through the signs with him, sounding out the words that were not in the language that his grandmother had spoken. Usually after Ćimbai had said a word a number of times, in varying intonations, Geirr was able to guess what it was. It was like divination. As all David's companions were underemployed, this process took on a fascination for everybody. For weeks, the horse pens were full of men in varying numbers, listening to Geirr figure out the words in the *qan*'s language, and then arguing about what they meant and how best to make them into phrases worthy of writing down. In due course, Athanasios would then write them down in Greek characters.

At first Eyvind had been unwilling to let the priest mark up his parchment. He felt that it would look messy, disturbing the handsome design, and wondered if it might compromise whatever spells the text contained. Geirr had persuaded him otherwise. The boy wanted his work recognized, all this strange labour of interpreting sounds and making words and statements. This desire was something Eyvind could respect. The priest also said to him, in his pompous way, "This is a barbarous tongue and nobody will ever be able to understand it if it is not written out in Greek. Who even knows what this language is? The speech of a few nomads? It will never amount to anything. Greek is the language of Alexander, who conquered half the world."

So the time passed. They made it through the ports that the Khazars still controlled, paying their tolls. Then they were in Garthariki, paying Rus tolls. More men who spoke the river-language came and went. More had light hair; Eyvind noticed that particularly. He had gotten used to feeling like the only dun or roan in a herd of black horses. Finally, Eyvind arrived at Helmgard, with his tottering horses, who had all survived. Eyvind had doubts about his chestnut colt, who was very weak, but thought that he might revive with a few weeks of feeding. It was high summer, three years since he had met David there in the first place. As Eyvind had dealt with the river transactions throughout the Rus lands, sparing the Khazar merchants higher tolls and trouble, they parted on good terms. Each had been of use to the other. "I left with a stripling and came back with a magician," said David, clapping him on the shoulder.

"But a pagan, still," said Eyvind, "you see that Athanasios did not manage to convert me."

"There was never any danger of that," replied David.

––––––––––––

It took Eyvind and the horses another year to return all the way to Iceland. He had to spend two months restoring them to health before allowing them to face another ship voyage. His young stallions were in bad shape. Mares are tougher. Once they had gained enough weight to stay alive, it was another long trip by water to Uppsala, followed by a hard trek in winter across Svealand and Norvegr. This they would never have survived but for the mare with no name. Lost in snow and wind and darkness, he would give the white mare her head and let her choose the direction. She unerringly picked the proper route. As she had never been to Iceland, or even to the port of Bergen, for which they were making, Eyvind had no idea how she could do this. She was like a migrating bird migrating to a wholly new place. The other animals followed her with blind conviction. This was not unusual in a herd with a senior mare—the colts were too young and too feeble from want to establish dominance—but her authority was absolute. Eyvind felt during this time that even he was her subject. He completed various tasks to preserve the horses, but the mare provided leadership. On a number of occasions in the freezing dark, just as a horse was about to pitch over a cliff or step on to rotten ice, or just as he himself was about to do so, Eyvind would hear the mare scream a warning. He always heard her perfectly, despite howling wind. He understood that this was impossible, and concluded therefore that he heard her with his deaf ear. He did not dwell on this observation as he was too busy trying to stay alive. They finally reached Bergen at the dawn of a still-brief day. Eyvind had never been so glad in his life, and, thanks to the mare, he still had twenty-one horses.

According to Eyvind, the mare had never been to Iceland, or to Bergen, yet she knew how to come there.

The one time that I ever left Iceland, to receive ordination at Nidaros, I, too, was lost in the terrible forests of the mainland. Trees are inimical to men. It has never surprised me that our grandparents Adam and Eve were brought low by the fruit of a tree. A forest at night, all whining whispers in a vile darkness without stars or horizon, is enough to strike terror into the heart of an Icelander. So it was with me, at least. Lost in the valley of Opdal among the black trunks of trees, hearing wolves howling, I said: "O blessed Thorlak, hear the prayer of your countryman Jór! Get me out of these woods!" Soon after that, light came down from a crack in the forest canopy and illuminated footsteps in the snow, leading away up the valley. They glowed slightly, these footsteps, and it came to me that they were the tracks of Thorlak, from the time when he himself went to Nidaros to be consecrated bishop. I stepped onto the track and felt immediately secure. Soon enough I was safe in the church at Vang. In my opinion Saint Thorlak led me through that wilderness in the same way that the mare with no name led Eyvind. Holy powers will sometimes intervene to get an Icelander where he needs to go.

In Iceland, Eyvind became a rich man. He sold most of the horses at high prices, keeping the white mare, his roan gelding, and the chestnut colt for himself. People paid enormous sums to get his horses once they understood how far they had come and what conditions they had survived. As he had named none of them, each family had the additional satisfaction of naming their own horses. They were all surprised that he had not done so and considered it somewhat callous. He told them that there was a prohibition against it where they had come from, but that they were Icelandic horses now. Their new owners were free to do as they pleased. People will pay a premium for this in Iceland.

The horses that Eyvind brought to Iceland were named Atorka, Bjarmi, Brúnlukka, Baldursbrá, Doppa, Faxa, Appal, Neista, Jarpstjarna, Valva, Grasa, Alftarleggur, Aleiga, Tóa, Ama, Aska, Birta, and Eyrar-Rauthur. Eleven of them had a natural tölt. Eyvind had picked them for this reason. His roan gelding had that gait and spending months in the saddle had taught him its value. The white mare had not shown it at all when he had first known her. Two herdsmen, admiring her greatly in all other respects, had discussed this single deficit as they drove her up into the highlands with the main herd during her first winter in Iceland. When spring came, she came down the mountain at a perfect tölt. She could even do the flying pace. She was not one ever to be outdone.

Eyvind had equal success with the *isgeir*. You will find this cloth in Iceland to this day. Persuading people to part with precious wool to make a new kind of fabric of which they had no knowledge was admittedly challenging at first. Women thought it was ridiculous that wool should not be spun. Old women suggested darkly that it was ungodly. Weaving was part of the order of things; it was wrong just to mash fibres together. So, some never took to felting, but those who did found it very useful, especially for saddles and boots. Eyvind, whose farm was on a windy headland, thought back fondly to the huge windbreaks made of *isgeir* that he had known in the *qan*'s country, great swathes of dense fabric staked deep into the ground to baffle the endless winds blowing across the steppes. Each one contained the wool of hundreds of sheep. But he could not see his way clear to such an expense.

Eyvind's farm was in Eyri, as you might have expected. A man will go back to his birthplace to show off the wealth he has made. It was a good farm. At one edge of it was a hot spring, where Eyvind had his bath and a place to cook bread. There, also, he often saw ghosts. As a rule he did not fear them. They were in a peaceable mood and had come to get warm. It is less trouble if ghosts come to your bath than your house, as you are not expending fuel

on them. He told a number of them whom he encountered on a regular basis that they were free to use it when
he was not there. This seemed to satisfy them. People,
whether living or dead, require clarity about matters of
property. Very occasionally a ghost would steal his bread,
if he left it there too long. On a couple of occasions he
went so far as to threaten them with a door-court, then
left them for a couple of days to wrangle among themselves. The threat of being charged with trespass and los-
ing a comfortable situation was always effective. They
would apologize about the bread and assure him that better discipline would be kept. One ghost named Thorir,
punctilious by nature, offered to replace it. Eyvind was
pleased at this offer but declined, thinking that the bread
of the dead was unlikely to be wholesome.

Eyvind brought three treasures back from his journey:
the horses, the *isgeir*, and the boy, Geirr. Geirr proved to
be a talented man. He was useful on the farm. He was
a superb horseman, much in demand as a trainer and a
race-rider. Unlike Eyvind, he had the gift of extemporiz-
ing poetry. He was good at flyting and improvising scurrilous verses, those forms which were appropriate to men
of his rank. He had also made for himself with great skill
a two-string fiddle that he called an *ikil*, strung with horse
hair. These abilities made him popular at any kind of fes-
tival. Though he was small and dark, he was extremely

attractive to women. By the time he was nineteen he had fathered two sons. Fortunately for Eyvind, neither of these occasioned any legal charges. Neither woman claimed to have been raped by him and little money had to change hands. The mother of the first child, whom Eyvind ironically chose to name Eylimi when he took him into his house, was a bondswoman from a moderately well-off family whom Geirr had met when he and Eyvind attended the Althing. The family did not want to keep the boy but allowed the mother to look after him until he was weaned for a small fee. Thereafter Eylimi lived on the farm in Eyri.

The second paternity case was more complicated. Its effects were far-reaching. Geirr had met a woman named Thorgunna at a horse race. She was from the Suthreyar, a freed bondswoman who had earned her way out by fine weaving. She was considerably older than Geirr. Indeed, she had considered herself past the child-bearing years, and possibly barren, as she had no other children. So she slept with Geirr when he asked her. He was very flattering. At this time his son Eylimi was six months old. When Geirr came to Eyvind, shamefaced, and admitted that he had fathered another child, Eyvind was not pleased. After his anger had passed, however, he asked to meet Thorgunna. She was seven months pregnant at that time and supported herself by weaving. Eyvind was impressed by her independence. After much negotiation, this is what transpired: Thorgunna came to live at the farm in Eyri, as housekeeper and wet-nurse. She would look after her own child and the infant Eylimi. She also brought her loom, a valuable item which had taken her many years to earn. She would thus be worth her keep and more. Eyvind had no wife. The prospect of a feminine hand in arranging domestic life was a welcome one. Geirr was relieved. He had been afraid that Eyvind was going to throw him out of his house, and instead he had been extraordinarily accommodating. The fact was that Eyvind loved Geirr like a son.

It was clear to Eyvind by this time that Hoë'lün's magic had not worked, and that he would have no natural sons or grandsons. The children of Geirr were thus the only ones he would ever have in his house. A farmer needs men to work. A man needs someone to inherit his land. And the fact is that children are enlivening. No farm without them is a pleasant place. So Eyvind was prepared to settle down with this odd family arrangement, even if it was not very respectable. He was not a chieftain or a gothi. No childless man ever became either. But it was his farm, and on it he could do what he pleased.

However, what Eyvind pleased did not, in the end, please Geirr. Geirr was not a resentful man by nature, but nor was he steady. He could not keep his mind on one thing for long.

He was too young to settle down with a woman and two children. Thorgunna was a strong-willed person who spoke her mind. Eyvind found, to his surprise, that he liked this about her. She reminded him of Hoë'lün. But by the time Eylimi and his younger brother Eír—so-called because he had inherited his father's copper complexion—were entering their third year, Geirr was fed up. He became difficult to live with. He and Thorgunna were estranged. Eyvind began asking around about raiding or trading expeditions. Finally, he found one. Geirr joined a party that was setting off to expand the new colony in Groenland. Land was fertile there and wildlife more abundant. It was a more adventurous setting for a young man, where he could fish and trap, or farm. And, thought Eyvind, any further children that Geirr fathered at that distance would be his own problem. Nonetheless, he gave Geirr two fine sheep and two horses, a young dun stallion and a grey filly, both offspring of the white mare. "The horses ought to bring you luck," he said to Geirr. "You have a certain kinship."

"I will not name them," said Geirr, smiling. He thanked Eyvind sincerely for his gifts, said farewell to Thorgunna and his sons, and left. Upon leaving he spoke this poem, "Horse-Head Fiddle":

> *Male string, female string;*
> *Bow struck, one song:*

Two sons. Blood and milk
Are just as strong.

Father of none, father of all:
Island wind that passes through.
Only empty walls resound
Where sons not born are found.

"He will impregnate half the women of Groenland," said Thorgunna.

"Let him, so long as I don't have to look after them," replied Eyvind.

———————

Eyvind and Thorgunna stayed on the farm in Eyri, and prospered. The two Geirssons grew up to be fine men, though they looked nothing alike. Eylimi was fair and Eír dark. They became excellent farmers. Thorgunna, once she was less busy raising the boys, returned to working with her loom. People brought spun wool and flax to her from all over Eyri. She made good money, so the family was never short of butter and cheese. She also became an expert with *isgeir*. People all over Iceland coveted her saddle cloths, which she sold occasionally at the festivities surrounding the Althing.

Like many women from the Suthreyar, Thorgunna was prophetic. She did not make a big fuss about it and nor did Eyvind. As he always said, for various reasons he had become used to uncanny women. One evening she came out to call him in to the evening meal. The white mare was there with her newest colt. Thorgunna touched her neck. Thereafter she was silent for a long time. That night, as Eylimi and Eír were in their bed and the two of them in theirs, she said: "You, Eyvind, are a barren man who yet has two sons; you perform *seithr*. You and your life are far from nothing. But that mare whom you have brought to Iceland, she who has no name, this I can tell you about her. Nearly a thousand years from now, this island explodes in blood and fire. Almost all the horses die. And those who live, every single one, are her descendants, the horses of magic and wisdom and luck. And in the ash and darkness of the succeeding time, there are just enough horses and just enough men for life to go on here. Just enough."

Some three hundreds of years, I estimate, have passed since Eyvind of Eyri made his journey to the country of the *qan*. There are still plenty of horses and plenty of men in Iceland. Nonetheless, it is appropriate that

Thorgunna's prophecy be recorded, lest it ever be fulfilled. There is no reason to suppose that God could not inspire a person living at that time, as he did in the age of the Old Testament. I myself am a man of Eyri, and thus I feel kinship for Eyvind, though he can be no forefather of mine. But when I left the farm at Helgafell to train as a priest at Skálaholt, I rode on a white mare under a saddle of felt.

Acknowledgments

I have to acknowledge here the huge help given to me by my husband, Scott-Morgan Straker, with sources in Old Norse, and the thesis work of his former student, Dr. Matthew Roby, on ghosts in the saga literature.

Notes on Names, Sources, and Poetic Forms

Everything about this story is fictional. Nonetheless, anyone who is familiar with *Eyrbyggja saga, Grettirs saga, The Secret History of the Mongols,* the Schechter Document, the travelogue of Ahmad Ibn Fadlan, the purported letters between Hasdai ibn Shaprut and Joseph of Khazaria, or the modern English ghazals of Shahid Ali Khan will recognize elements of it. I apologize to people who read the languages in all disciplines related to these works for the use of place and personal names dropped in to contemporary English without inflections, and for anachronism in using words from modern Turkish and Mongolian to represent their ninth-century counterparts. This story takes place in the early ninth century, before written literacy in Iceland or Mongolia, and during the period in which the Khazar Khaganate was still powerful, though we have few records of it now, and no samples of the language other than toponyms. I treat the story of the Jews of Khazaria as a wonder tale. Other writers have treated it in other ways. I also avoid using the words *Viking* or *shaman,* both of which are often used irresponsibly, in my opinion. Events imagined here also pre-date the foundation narrative of the Kievan Rus *Primary Chronicle*. Oleg and Olga of Novgorod (Helmgard) are not meant to refer to historical people. I assume that Garthariki, the territory controlled by the Rus, contained a mixed Norse and Slavic culture and have indicated this in the river-language that Eyvind and his fellow traders speak, a form of Norse-Slavic creole. Personal and tribe names from *The Secret History of the Mongols* likewise should not be taken to refer to historical individuals in the lineage of Genghis Khan.

The ghazal has a rich history and this tale pre-dates most of it as a written form. I read none of the languages in which it was developed. The form in which it occurs here, in Ibrahim's poem, uses the technique of Shahid Ali Khan in rendering the monorhyme of the ghazal into English, as I encountered it in his book *Call Me Ishmael Tonight*. Among other things that this story is meant to gesture towards speculatively is what the Persian-Arabic encounter that was the origin of the ghazal as a lyric form might have been, in exactly this period, and in a place as mysterious as Khazaria, namely Khwarazem. This region, south of the Aral Sea (The Sea of Islands) in what is now Uzbekistan, is famous as the birthplace of the polymath Al-Biruni and of the mathematician Abū Jafar Mohammad ibn Musa, from whose cognomen al-Kwārizmī we get the word *algorithm*. The poem uttered by Geirr is a *lausavisa*, an isolated and topical lyric poem or stanza such as often occur in Norse sagas. These are usually *drottkvaet*. Let's face it; his poem is not one. It suggests one in having eight short lines with considerable assonance and alliteration, and in having a riddling quality that suggests kennings, but that is probably blown in including the title "Horse-Head Fiddle." The instrument that Geirr constructs is the two-string Mongolian *ikil* or *morin khuur*.

The incident foretold by Thorgunna is the fissure eruption of June 8, 1783, in the southern district of Sitha, that resulted in the formation of the Laki chain of volcanoes. It continued for eight months, devastated livestock and people in Iceland, and changed the world's weather until at least 1785. That the mare with no name could be the traceable single ancestor of all Icelandic horses since that time is genetically possible, though, of course, still fictional.

ST

About the Author

Scott Straker

SARAH TOLMIE is the author of the Tordotcom novella *The Fourth Island* (2020). With McGill-Queen's University Press, she has published the poetry collections *Check* (2020) and *The Art of Dying* (2018), as well as the 120-sonnet sequence *Trio* (2015). In 2014, she published the chapbook *Sonnet in a Blue Dress and Other Poems* (Baseline Press). She has two novels with Aqueduct Press, *The Little Animals* (2019) and *The Stone Boatmen* (2014), as well as the short fiction collections *Disease* (2020), *Two Travelers* (2016), and *NoFood* (2014). She is a medievalist trained at the University of Toronto and Cambridge and is a professor of English at the University of Waterloo.

TOR·COM

**Science fiction. Fantasy. The universe.
And related subjects.**

*

More than just a publisher's website, *Tor.com*
is a venue for **original fiction, comics,** and
discussion of the entire field of SF and fantasy,
in all media and from all sources. Visit our site
today—and join the conversation yourself.